A lis...

It seemed to me that I was looking at a list. A list of names.

Remembering Potsy's still, waxen-faced body lying beside the wheels of the shuttle bus, and Bob's blood-chilling scream as the lawn mower sliced away at his feet, my teeth began chattering.

Because I knew then, as surely as I knew my own name, that what I was looking at was a list of *victims*. And I could be next.

Terrifying thrillers by Diane Hoh:

NIGHTMARE HALL

DIANE HOH

Discovery Middle School
Instructional Materials Center
Granger, Indiana

SCHOLASTIC INC.
New York Toronto London Auckland Sydney

ISBN 0-590-25082-5

12 11 10 9 8 7 6 5 4 3 2 1   5 6 7 8 9/9 0/0

Printed in the U.S.A.   01

First Scholastic printing, August 1995

Prologue

Finished.

Done.

All of it down in black and white.

Victims' names.

Dates of execution.

Methods of execution.

All there. In a special code, of course. No one will ever figure it out. Even with the code, it could mean disaster if anyone else got their hands on the disk.

And this, of course, is only for the first four victims. There will be more. Many more. If Phase I is a success, and why wouldn't it be, Phase II will follow.

The mission now is to see the plan through, exactly as it's written down in the Death file.

Time to Save the file. REDD, I've titled it. For REVENGE and DEAD. Revenge is my goal, Dead is what they'll all be, each and every one of them. REDD.

Save file. There, that's done!

Close file. Done.

Exit file. Done.

Exit . . . I like that word. If all goes well, more than just the file will exit. Four people on this campus will exit as well. Forever.

They deserve to die for what they've done.

Can't be soon enough. Had to be patient for too long. But no more. It's time now.

Save.

Close.

Exit.

Chapter 1

I couldn't have said afterwards exactly how it happened.

I was standing on campus in front of the science building in a crowd waiting for the Salem University shuttle bus that takes us into town, and should have been a good eyewitness. I was right there, so I should have been able to answer all of the questions that came up later. But I couldn't.

Because I was daydreaming, as usual. First, I was wishing I'd taken Esmerelda off campus instead of waiting for the shuttle. Essie was my very own secondhand Pontiac sedan. She'd been a boring navy-blue when I got her, two years ago on my sixteenth birthday. Now she was canary yellow, and decorated with small white daisies with orange centers. I hand-painted them myself, and I did a great job, if I do say so.

Essie was my most prized possession. My *only* prized possession. I regretted spurning her for the shuttle. I was taking the bus to save on gas. But I hadn't expected such a long wait.

I was also thinking about the tall, interesting-looking guy who was standing in front of me, a little to my right. I was arguing with myself, telling myself that I wasn't the least bit interested in dating anyone right now, because I was just beginning my college career. I knew the work was going to be harder than in high school. And I was never a straight-A student. I would have to concentrate really hard to get the grades I wanted. So I shouldn't even be looking at guys.

Besides, I was still stinging from my disastrous relationship with Brigham. I'd been burned. Third-degree, head to toe. Why walk straight into the fire again so soon?

Nevertheless, I couldn't resist glancing at this guy every now and then. It wasn't just his looks that intrigued me, although they were okay. Everything was in the right place and nicely sculpted, and I liked the way the brown hair was summer-streaked. I was looking at a strong intelligent face, one that looked as if it could be trusted. But then, I'd thought that about Brigham, too, hadn't I? And I'd been wrong.

What interested me most about him wasn't his looks. It was the way he was talking animatedly to Brynne Sawyer. Lucky Brynne. The guy had a disarming grin and used it a lot, as if he were poking fun at himself. As if, in spite of the way tall, gorgeous, red-haired Brynne was hanging on his every word, he knew it was all nonsense and was trying to warn her not to take him so seriously. He shrugged several times, as if to say, "Hey, what do I know, anyway?"

I liked that.

So, although I could have given every detail about the kind of day it was and how beautiful the campus looked in early autumn, I couldn't say specifically, precisely, exactly what happened at the curb . . . because I had been daydreaming.

"Addie, put your eyes back in your head," my roommate, Shelley Karlsen, ordered. She was standing at my elbow. "I admit he's not bad-looking, but you're going to drill a hole in his forehead if you keep staring like that."

I tore my eyes away. "I wasn't . . ."

"Yeah, you were. He's not your type. He's one of those everybody-loves-me-because-I-deserve-it guys. I can almost hear him thinking, Those two girls over there, the tall, thin one and the short, dumpy one, want to join my fan club. Are they worthy?"

Shelley isn't dumpy. She used to be. But not anymore.

I looked at her in surprise. "You know that guy?"

"I don't have to. High school was full of guys like him. They strolled through the corridors like monarchs inspecting their kingdoms. I know one when I see one."

"Shelley! You just admitted that you don't even know the guy. Now you're analyzing him as if you're a shrink and he's your patient. He doesn't look like that kind of person at all. Don't you think you're being a little unfair?"

"Nope." Shelley is short and since she lost a lot of weight last year, is almost as thin as me. But her opinions are as strong and sturdy as ever. We've known each other for eight years. Shelley's personality is, well, let's say, commanding. Very commanding. She always sounds so certain about everything. It's hard to argue with her. "I call them the way I see them. Anyway, did you or did you not swear after Brigham that you were never, ever going to fall in love again? Didn't I, as your best friend and constant companion, hear those words from your very own lips at least a hundred times?"

Talking about Brigham made me uncomfortable, so I lifted my head and pretended I was scanning the wide, rolling green of campus for some sign of the yellow shuttle bus. "I didn't *say* I was in love with the guy," I protested, whispering because the crowd was pressing in on me and I was terrified that the guy I had been staring at would overhear our conversation and guess that he was the subject. If that happened, I would die. "I just think he's interesting-looking, that's all. And you don't even know him, so just muzzle up, okay?"

"He's Donovan McGarry," Shelley said abruptly.

I stared at her. "You *do* know him!"

"Not really. But I know he's Donovan McGarry. He's in my math class. Very, very smart." Shelley grinned. "You two probably have nothing in common. You never got anything above a C in math in your life."

Absolutely true. But not something I was proud of, so I didn't appreciate her announcing it like that. "I got straight A's in English all through high school," I said defensively.

"He's looking at you, Addie. And dear, sweet Brynnie doesn't look too happy about it. I thought she was dating Kirk Howard. Maybe that look on her face means she can't understand why a guy would be looking at you when he could be looking at her gorgeous face."

Involuntarily, my eyes shot over to the couple. Shelley was right. Donovan McGarry was looking at me, and Brynne absolutely did not look pleased.

I was embarrassed, and looked away quickly.

"Good girl," Shelley approved. "No point in encouraging him. Besides, you don't want to make Brynne your enemy. Not a good idea."

I didn't think there was much chance of Donovan McGarry or anyone else picking long-legged, awkward Addie Adair, with long, wildly frizzy hair of no specific color, just a mishmash of browns and reds and dull gold, over Brynne Sawyer's obvious perfection. Although my eyes are a stunning, if I do say so myself, shade of blue, and I guess I have a pretty nice smile.

Still, I'd never be on the cover of a magazine, never date a rock star or famous professional athlete, never win Homecoming Queen.

"Here they come!" Shelley hissed suddenly, yanking on the elbow of my white sweater. I heard a ripping sound, and looked down in dismay. There was a hole the size of a quarter in my sweater.

"Shelley! Look what you did!"

But Brynne was already saying "hi" in a pleasant enough tone of voice. It was her eyes that gave her away. They were a deep, true green, but I'd never seen them quite that cold before. Kind of like jade. Personally, I thought she was almost too pretty for her own good. Perfect skin, perfect hair, perfect mouth. All that perfection had to be a pain sometimes. But then, maybe I felt that way because perfection was something I knew so little about.

"Addie Adair, freshman, English Lit major, the Quad," Brynne said, "meet Donovan McGarry, freshman, majoring in electronics engineering, whatever that is, lives at Nightmare Hall."

I said hi. "Nightmare Hall?"

"Nightingale Hall, actually. Off-campus dorm, down the road," Donovan answered, waving his hand in that direction. "Big, gloomy brick house, up on a hill overlooking the highway. You must have seen it on your way into town."

"Oh. That place." I knew it and couldn't repress an involuntary shiver of distaste. So dark, so shadowed by all those old trees surrounding it. I couldn't imagine actually living in such a creepy place. "You *live* there?"

He laughed. "People *do* live there. That's

why it's called an off-campus dorm. It's cheap, convenient, and the housemother is a cream puff. Is Addie your real name?"

Ignoring that question, I asked one of my own. "Why do they call it Nightmare Hall? I mean, besides the way it looks?"

Brynne answered for him. "Partly, like Donovan said, because it's so ominous-looking. Those twisted, old oaks look like giant monsters hovering over the house. But they also call it that because someone died there. Maybe even more than one person, for all I know. I've been hearing stories about that place ever since I hit campus. I wouldn't go near it if you paid me." She smiled up at Donovan. "You must be really brave."

Shelley rolled her eyes at me.

"Oh, I am brave," Donovan said with mock gravity. "I don't quake in my boots at the thought of a dentist's drill, I once killed an attacking mosquito with my bare hand, and I'm not afraid to ask Addie Adair here if she'd like to take in a movie tonight, in spite of the fact that she still hasn't told me what her real name is."

He said all of that so fast that he caught me off guard and all I could stammer was, "Adelaide. It's Adelaide."

Shelley shoved an elbow into my ribs. Remember Brigham, it warned.

"But I can't go to a movie," I added hastily. "I'm sorry. I have an English paper due on Monday. Have to work in the computer lab tonight." And I'm not as brave as you are, I added silently. Never have been. I do quake at the thought of a dental drill, I'm terrified of bees and hornets, and most important of all, relationships scare me half to death. *You*, Donovan McGarry, scare me half to death. Aloud, I said, "Maybe some other time?"

"Yeah, sure. Whatever." But he looked disappointed, and his hazel eyes looked suspicious of the computer lab excuse.

Well, it *was* only Friday afternoon. I had just admitted that the paper wasn't due until Monday, which meant that I had the whole weekend to finish it. He knew that. He'd probably never ask me out again.

Good. If I dated anyone at all at Salem, it was going to be someone ugly and stupid and boring. That way, I couldn't possibly get hurt . . . again.

Donovan McGarry didn't seem dumb or stupid or boring. So I wouldn't be dating him, period.

"Where *is* that stupid shuttle?" Brynne complained. Now that I'd turned Donovan down, her eyes weren't quite as dark green. "I thought it was supposed to run every fifteen minutes. We've been waiting longer than that."

Brynne wasn't the only one complaining. The crowd, too, was becoming impatient. The pushing and shoving began to worsen, which made no sense to me, since the bus wasn't even in sight.

When it became apparent that the crowd had become too large to fit into one small shuttle bus, people began pushing harder to get as close to the front as possible. No one wanted to be left behind to wait for another bus.

In the front row, closest to the curb, I saw two boys from my math class. I didn't know their names, although one looked vaguely familiar. They seemed to be jockeying for position at the curb.

"We're going to miss the beginning of the movie!" a girl near the rear of the crowd wailed. "I hate walking in in the middle, especially when it's a thriller."

Maybe she was the one who started the newest surge toward the front. Or it could have been someone else headed for the same movie at the mall.

"There's the bus!" Donovan McGarry said from behind me, where he was standing with

Brynne. When I turned to look, I saw that they'd been joined by the boy she'd been dating, Kirk Howard. A big, burly guy, massive from the waist up, dark, shaggy hair, very good-looking, just the type I'd expect Brynne to be attracted to.

When Donovan pointed out the approaching bus, half of the crowd rushed forward, away from the yellow sign reading SHUTTLE STOP, as if by making a dash to meet the bus halfway, they'd be assured of a seat.

"Now there's a dumb move if I ever saw one," Kirk Howard remarked. "The drivers never stop until they're right underneath the sign. They're all going to have to turn around and race back up here, anyway. They'll end up on the end of the line, after all, and have to wait for another bus. Serves them right for being so pushy."

"They're defeating their purpose," Donovan agreed. "But let's not tell them that, okay?" He laughed. "It'll leave more seats for the rest of us."

"Maybe not," Shelley said, and began moving forward. "There are so many of them, the bus just might stop when it sees them, thinking they're standing in the right place. If he does pick them up there, we'll never get a seat. Come on, you guys, I don't want to have to stand here another fifteen minutes."

Brynne agreed, and began dragging Kirk after Shelley. They joined the splinter group and began pushing their way to the front. Donovan shrugged and followed.

I thought what they were doing was a colossal waste of time. The bus wouldn't stop until it got to the sign. It never did. But I didn't want to be left behind, alone. So I gave in and followed, too.

I was still struggling through the crowd to catch up to Shelley and the others, when the fat little yellow bus pulled left off the highway onto Campus Drive. It was moving swiftly toward the sign designating its precise stopping point.

I remember the bus advancing rapidly toward us, and I remember people in the front of the crowd craning their necks and leaning forward, as if by doing so, they'd be boarding first.

And the my thoughts returned to Donovan McGarry and I asked myself why I had turned him down when I had the whole weekend to finish my English paper. It wasn't as if guys were falling at my feet begging me to date them.

If I hadn't let myself be distracted by Donovan, I might have seen exactly what happened next. It wasn't as if my eyes were closed. They were wide open. But not seeing.

So all I could say later, when I was asked, was, "They were all just starting to run back toward the bus stop. I was in the middle of the crowd and couldn't see what was happening up front and I wasn't really paying attention, anyway. I saw the bus slow down, swinging in toward the curb, but you could see that it wasn't going to stop until it got to the sign, so everyone started running back that way. It was just one big mess, with people pushing and shoving and yelling. Then, I saw arms waving. There was something weird about the way the arms waved in the air. They were waving the way people do when they're falling, frantically trying to grab something to hold onto to stop them from falling.

"And then I heard the agonizing screech of brakes. It seemed to go on forever. It sounded horrible, like a whole bunch of cats fighting.

"When that sound finally stopped, there was just one tiny second of complete, utter silence, as if everyone in the crowd had stopped breathing.

"Then all at once, people started gasping and screaming and shouting and crying. The people toward the front were looking down at something in the road. I couldn't see what it was, but I saw one girl turn around, her hands at her face, and she was crying. So I knew something really terrible had happened.

"The people still standing beneath the yellow sign began to move then, rushing forward in one big, thick pack."

That was what I told the police I had seen. They said, "Thank you very much, miss, for your help," but I knew they were disappointed. I hadn't been any help.

I should have been paying more attention.

I finally pushed my way through to the front. Shelley, Brynne, Donovan, and Kirk stood off to one side on the edge of the curb, looking down. I pushed through to them and followed their eyes.

The bus driver, in his frantic attempt to stop when he realized what had happened, had skidded the bus sideways and it now sat at a right angle to the curb.

And beside it, lying parallel to the curve of the front wheels, lay one of the boys from my math class.

He was lying on his stomach, his jeans splayed out lifelessly, as if they had no legs inside them. A tire mark was clearly visible on his back, undulating black waves drawn across a white T-shirt. His head was turned sideways, toward the crowd. Toward us. His eyes were open, but unseeing. A thin stream of bright red trailed from his open mouth, another from his ear.

Beneath his head, a larger pool of vivid scarlet began to spread across the gray pavement.

Chapter 2

I couldn't take in what I was seeing. Someone I knew, however slightly, was lying in the road at my feet, bleeding. Maybe dead. But I felt nothing. Everything around me, the screaming, the shouting, the crying, the smell of burned rubber from the driver's valiant attempt to prevent disaster, the broken figure beside the bus, all of it seemed unreal, as if I were watching it on television.

But it was all real.

Someone ran for help. Someone else threw a lightweight jacket over the victim. The bus driver, a middle-aged, overweight man in a red shirt, leaned against the front of the bus, his face gray, saying in a stunned voice, "He came out of nowhere, just fell right in front of the bus, I tried to stop in time, but I couldn't, there was no way, no way . . ."

The truth of what was taking place swept

over me. Nausea shot up from my stomach to my throat, and I could feel myself swaying on the curb.

Shelley was at my side then, saying, "Addie? Addie, are you okay? I know it's horrible, it's awful. Just don't look, okay? Come on, let's get out of here. They don't need us. We can't help. Let's go, all right?"

"She okay?" a short, good-looking boy with curly blond hair asked Shelley. I'd never seen him before, but she seemed to know him.

"She'll be fine, Cam, thanks for asking," she said. "I can handle it."

The boy nodded and turned away.

"Cameron Truro," Shelley said, although I couldn't have cared less. "That's his jacket on the ground there." I could tell she didn't want to say the word "victim." "He tossed it over the guy the minute he saw what had happened. Come on, let's go."

I tore my eyes away, then, from the figure lying underneath Cameron Truro's pale blue windbreaker. All around me people were crying, whispering, or standing pale and silent, their eyes fixed on the figure in the road, just as mine had been. "Go? Go where?" It didn't seem right to leave. Not while he was lying there, helpless and bleeding.

My eyes returned reluctantly to the victim.

The pool of red beneath his head had widened. His skin, on the upturned side of his face, was white and waxy, like the cold, marble floor in the entrance to the campus library.

"What happened?" someone cried. "Did he fall?"

Someone else shouted, "Why wasn't he watching where he was going? He shouldn't have been rushing like that, just to get a seat on the bus."

And then the police showed up and asked all of us questions.

No one had any answers. No one knew exactly what happened.

"He shouldn't have been pushing like that," people kept murmuring, as if by blaming the victim for his carelessness, they could dismiss the whole thing.

Each time I heard someone say it, I nodded, in a daze.

Someone touched my elbow. I looked up. It was Donovan McGarry, with Kirk on one side of him, and a white-faced Brynne on the other.

"Addie?" Donovan said. "Shelley's right, Addie. We need to go. We can't do anything here." To Shelley he said quietly, "Maybe we should take her to the infirmary. I think she's in shock."

If there is one thing I can't stand, it's being

talked about in the third person as if I'm no-where in sight. My older sister, Mary, and her husband Stokes, do it to me all the time. I live with them when I'm not in school. "The school called again," Mary would say when Stokes walked in the door at night after a day in the city doing something with stocks and bonds. "She's not doing her math homework."

Stokes would shrug and say, "Well, we can't very well strap her to a chair and tie a pencil to her fingers, now can we? If she doesn't want to do it, we can't make her."

And Mary's response was always the same. Right in front of me she'd say, "Mother and Dad were both teachers. They'd roll over in their graves if they knew the kind of grades she's bringing home, except for English and speech. And gym! And it's embarrassing for me. I *teach* at that school, Stokes! How do you think it makes me feel when my own sister, someone I'm responsible for, deliberately sab-otages her chances of getting into college?"

Mary, a lifelong straight-A student, never understood that my academic struggles weren't deliberate sabotage. Were *not*. I *wanted* to go to college. Anything to get out of that house and away from Miss Polly Perfect. Mary Adair, older sister and legal guardian of Adelaide Adair, had never screwed up in her life. Living with such an icon twenty-four hours a day was like having your fingernails ripped out slowly, one by one. I was so desperate to get out, I probably would have been dumb enough to marry Brigham, if he'd asked. But he hadn't. Not even close.

Still, Mary's lack of understanding wasn't half as crazy-making as her habit of talking about me as if I weren't around, when I was sitting right there, in plain sight of everyone in the room.

When Donovan did the same thing, anger sliced through my shock like a sharp knife. "I do *not* need to go to the infirmary," I said, my voice icy. "Look around you, do you see *anyone* who doesn't look as if they're in shock? Except for you four," I couldn't help adding caustically. "You all seem to be handling things really, really well."

"What's that supposed to mean?" Brynne snapped. "We're not screaming hysterically, so we're not upset? We don't have feelings? Is that what you're saying?"

"Hey, take it easy," Kirk Howard said. "Addie . . ." He glanced at me. "It *is* Addie, right?" When I nodded, he continued. "Addie didn't mean anything. She's upset, that's all."

But I *had* meant something. Shelley was pale, but seemed calm. Donovan wasn't even pale. Brynne looked as beautifully composed as she always did and clearly hadn't shed a tear. And Kirk seemed more concerned with keeping the peace than with the victim lying in the road.

"Hey, come on, guys," Shelley appealed. "Whether we show it or not, everyone's upset. Can't we just get out of here?"

"I don't even know what happened," I heard myself saying in a bewildered voice. "Did any of you see? You were closer to the front than I was. You must have seen."

They all shook their heads no.

Shelley said, "I'm *glad* I didn't see. Who wants to see someone crushed by a bus? If I had seen it, I'd have nightmares for the rest of my life. I guess he just fell. I almost fell myself, people were pushing so hard. As if the ship were sinking and they were desperate to reach the lifeboats. It really was disgusting."

Shelley was wrong. She wouldn't have had nightmares. Not her, I contradicted silently as an ambulance shrieked up to the scene. Shelley was too practical to have bad dreams. Or good dreams. Or even daydreams.

Shelley's mother had run off with an accountant named Dennis in the summer before we started our junior year. Her father had been devastated and Shelley, with two younger brothers, had had to grow up quickly. She never blamed her mother. She blamed Dennis, for taking her mother away, and her father, for not stopping them. She promptly put on twenty extra pounds after her mother left and kept them on until late fall of senior year. I knew it was to keep boys away from her. By the time she lost the weight, after Halloween of our last year at Wickley Adams Consolidated High, every male on that campus knew that Shelley had nothing but contempt for boys, romance, poetry, roses, Valentine's Day, and love songs. I saw plenty of guys eyeing her in the cafeteria and the library, at football and basketball games, at parties, but none of them had the courage to ask her out. They knew Shelley Karlsen no longer believed in happily-ever-afters and had little patience with those who did.

I'd been one of those believers . . . until Brigham cheated on me.

Although that whole stupid episode had taught me something, I wasn't anywhere near as cynical as Shelley was.

But then, my mother hadn't left me for an accountant. She and my father had died in a car crash. At least I knew they hadn't left me willingly.

Not only did Shelley not date, she didn't exactly rejoice when her friends dated, either.

My relationship with Brigham, beginning in June after our junior year, had given her a really hard time. All of a sudden, I wasn't there for her. She kept saying she was glad for me, but by late October of that year, when I was seeing Brigham almost every night and had hardly any time left over for Shelley, she had become really quiet and was biting her nails again.

When the thing with Brigham ended, Shelley said, "I always knew he wasn't good enough for you. You're better off without him."

They weren't very comforting words at the time.

In spite of her understandable cynicism, Shelley was a good friend. I figured one day she'd fall head over heels in love with some guy and change her tune.

Now we lingered just long enough to see the ambulance attendant shake his head grimly and hear a girl near the front of the crowd whisper, "Oh, no, he really is dead!"

Hearing it said aloud, pronounced with such conviction, stunned all of us anew. Another shocked hush fell over the crowd as the words were passed along. Dead. It seemed so harsh, said aloud like that. So final.

Dead.

"I didn't even know his name," I said softly

when we finally turned to leave. "He was in my math class, and he seemed nice, but I never asked him his name. He looked familiar, though. Sort of."

"I didn't get a good look at his face," Donovan said, "but he looked a little like a guy I went to high school with. Could have been. This is a big campus, and we haven't been here long enough to run into half the people on it."

"Did you know everyone you graduated with?" Brynne asked.

Donovan shook his head. "Not by a long shot. Big school." He glanced down at Brynne. "Could have graduated with *you* and might not have known it."

She laughed. "Get real, Donovan. You'd have known if I was in your class. I knew everyone I graduated with. A lot of them are right here on campus."

They made me sick. How could Brynne be laughing and flirting so soon after what happened? She didn't seem to care at all that someone who had been alive only a little while ago no longer was.

Kirk didn't look very happy with her, either, but I suspected that had nothing to do with the boy who had died. Probably had a lot more to do with the way Brynne was flirting with Donovan.

I had to get out of there. "I'm going to the computer lab," I said quietly. "See you people later." And ignoring Shelley's yelp of protest, which had something to do with eating, I hurried away.

My knees still felt mushy as I slid into a seat in one of the small computer cubicles in the library basement. I had my own computer in my dorm room, but I needed the research materials in the library.

I pulled the disk with my essay on it from my shoulder bag, switched on the computer, and slid the disk forward into the proper slot.

It wouldn't go in.

Surprised, I sat back in my chair, still holding the disk.

The trouble was, I really didn't care about it just then. English was my best subject, and I was counting on my usual good grade in there to boost my grade point average. But I was still so numb from what had happened, I couldn't concentrate on my schoolwork.

Why hadn't that guy from math class been more careful? He knew the bus was coming straight toward us. We'd all seen it. Why had he been teetering on the edge of the curb, so intent on getting a seat that he'd been careless?

I leaned forward to check the disk drive. My fingers encountered a small disk exactly like my own. Someone had left their disk in the computer.

I glanced around the white-walled cubicle, wondering if someone had been using the computer and had left it briefly to go get something, or maybe they were just taking a break.

No backpack, no books, no notebooks, no purse. The light hadn't even been on when I came in. I remembered turning it on. The computer had been off, too.

I pulled the disk free and glanced down at it, scanning it for a name, a title, something to tell me who it belonged to. The letters I saw written in black on the identifying label said REDD. That's all. Was that the name of the file? Or the name of its owner?

I didn't know anyone named Redd.

Well, whoever he or she was, if the disk was important, they'd come back for it. I set it aside, and then I slid my own disk into the computer and tried to work.

Impossible. Instead of my paper on the computer screen, I saw the yellow shuttle bus, and then arms flying out in desperation, then the body lying beside the wheels, and the tire marks waving across the white T-shirt. I saw the blood.

I'm *glad* I didn't see it happen, I told myself. Because I'm not like Shelley. I *would* have nightmares for the rest of my life. Probably would, anyway.

I tried half a dozen times to concentrate on my project, an analysis of *A Tale of Two Cities*, but each time, I saw again the upturned, waxen face. Dead. He was dead. In a matter of seconds, the life was crushed out of him.

Finally, I gave up. I yanked the stupid disk from the stupid computer and reached behind me for the shoulder bag I'd hung on the chair. The stupid strap had slipped free and the stupid bag was lying on the stupid floor.

And I hadn't been so angry in a long, long time. I wasn't even sure at what. The bus? The driver? The boy who had been so careless that he'd lost his life?

I turned off the computer and was bending to pick up my bag when a voice behind me said suddenly, "You look mad. You're not mad at me, are you? What'd I do?"

I almost fell off the chair. "Shelley! You scared me half to death! Don't ever sneak up on me like that!"

"Sorry. Thought you heard me coming."

I hadn't heard a thing. I'd been so lost inside my own head, I wouldn't have heard Shelley approaching if she'd been walking on bare hardwood in spike heels.

"We got an invite to eat at Burgers, Etc.

with Donovan and Brynne and Kirk," Shelley said as I swivelled around on my seat to face the door. "They're waiting for us over there. I thought it might be good for us. To be around people, I mean. If we go back to our room, we'll just brood. That's not healthy, right? Come on. It won't take long."

Burgers, Etc. was right across the road from campus. It was convenient, and it had the best burgers in the area. It was always crowded.

Did I really feel like being in a crowded restaurant now? Definitely not. But I wasn't getting any work done, and I knew Shelley was right. Going back to the room was definitely a bad idea.

I have low blood sugar, and need to eat regularly. Mary, my sister, hammered that into me for so long, I finally got it. I'm pretty careful now. Maybe if I ate something, I'd be able to concentrate again, and I would get something done before I went to bed.

"Okay," I said, sighing and plucking my shoulder bag off the floor. I slid my disk into my purse and stood up. "I do have the rest of the weekend to finish this, but I should get something done on it tonight. Maybe I'll come back here later." I turned off the light as we left the cubicle. "But why did they invite us? Brynne's the only one in that group that we know, and we don't even know her that well."

"How should I know? Maybe because we were all together there at the bus stop. Maybe seeing something so awful bonds people or something, in a weird sort of way. Anyway, they asked, and I said yes. You're not mad, are you?"

"No. I do need to eat, and I probably wouldn't have if you hadn't come and dragged me out of there."

"Well, there's nothing we can do for that poor guy now," Shelley said in her usual pragmatic way. "So we might as well go and eat. I don't see anything wrong with that, do you?"

No, I didn't. Not with life being much too short.

Chapter 3

Shelley was annoyed when we walked into Burgers, Etc. and found no one waiting for us. "They said they'd be here," she complained, glancing around the noisy, crowded diner with its blue plastic booths and tabletop miniature jukeboxes. Waitresses in blue and white uniforms dashed past us, trays in hand, and the cook at the grill behind the counter barked orders.

"Can we just sit down, please?" I begged, moving down the narrow aisle toward one of two available booths in the back.

We'd been sitting and talking for about fifteen minutes when Shelley's tone of voice changed as she looked up and cried, "Well, finally! Where have you guys been? I thought you were coming straight here."

Brynne breathed in deeply as she arrived at

the booth. "Umm, what a heavenly smell! I'm starving!" She slid in beside Shelley, and was quickly followed by Kirk Howard.

Donovan McGarry smiled at me as he took the remaining half of my seat. I didn't smile back. I didn't feel like smiling.

"So?" Shelley pressed. "Where were you?"

She received three different answers. Kirk had stopped at the library to return an overdue book. Brynne had gone to her room to get a sweater. "It's cooling off out there and I don't look good in goosebumps." And Donovan said he had stayed behind to find out who the victim was.

"Who was it?" Shelley asked bluntly.

Donovan shook his head. "Don't know. He was already inside the ambulance, so I never got a good look at him. If he was with friends, they'd already left, and the policemen on the scene said they weren't releasing his name until his family had been notified."

It was hard to pay attention to the conversation flowing around me. Kirk Howard saw someone he'd gone to high school with sitting in another booth and when he mentioned it, Donovan started talking about some guys he ran around with in senior year. When Brynne started a long, convoluted story about a girl who had been her rival in track in high school, I tuned out. None of it seemed important, after what had happened.

Donovan McGarry turned to me then and said, "Anyone from your high school here on campus, Addie?"

"Just Shelley, as far as I know," I answered. "There might be others, but I haven't run into them yet." And didn't really want to. I hadn't exactly distinguished myself in high school, and I didn't want someone who knew that to show up and ruin my chances of establishing an entirely different persona in college.

Cameron Truro, the short, blond-haired boy who had given up his blue windbreaker to the bus accident victim, ambled over to our booth just then and everyone began talking about the accident.

I didn't want to hear it all again, so I decided to split. Saying I had a paper to work on, which was true, I tried to talk Shelley into leaving with me. But she was looking at Cameron with an expression I had never once, in the eight years that I'd known her, seen on her face. It reminded me of a little girl I'd seen at the mall once, staring into a shop window at a Barbie doll dressed in sequinned evening wear. She clearly wanted that doll more than anything in the world, but the look on her face said she had no expectations of ever getting it. Shelley was looking at Cameron Truro in that same wistful way.

Shelley? And someone who looked like Truro?

Well, why not? Shelley was as cute as anyone. She had a wonderful, if biting, sense of humor, and she was loyal to the bone. The guy would be lucky to have such a person in his life.

As for Shelley, it was about time, if you asked me. She'd blamed the male gender for too long for her mother's abandonment. If she could get beyond that now, finally, with someone like this Truro guy, more power to her.

Donovan stood up to let me out of the booth. "Mind if I walk back with you?" he asked quietly.

I hadn't been expecting that. But it was dark outside and we'd all been warned at orientation not to walk across campus alone at night if we could help it. Part of some safety program or something. The instructor who'd conducted that particular part of orientation had hastily added that there was nothing to worry about, but there was safety in numbers, no sense taking chances, blah, blah, blah.

Since it was obvious when Cameron slid into Donovan's place in the booth that nothing short of shouting "Fire!" would have yanked Shelley out of that booth, I shrugged my shoulders casually and said, "Sure." I mean, it wasn't like he was taking me to dinner. We were just walking back to campus together, that was all. I figured when we got to the Quad, he'd go his way and I'd go mine.

When we got to the four tall, stone buildings linked together to make one massive dorm center, with the green, grassy Commons and its fountain in the center, Donovan insisted on walking me upstairs to my room. And since I'd felt fairly comfortable talking to him on the way back and we'd even laughed a little, I decided I wasn't quite ready to say good night and couldn't think of any reason why I should.

He waited in the hall while I opened the door. It wasn't locked, of course, in spite of the lecture on safety at orientation. I had enough trouble keeping track of books and purse and notebooks and assignments and my student ID and my wallet without having to remember where I'd put my room key. Usually, I left it on top of the dresser. Tonight was no exception.

"Shouldn't leave it unlocked like that," Donovan said, adding a smile so I wouldn't think he was criticizing me, which of course he was. "Weren't you listening at orientation?"

"I just forget sometimes, that's all. No big

deal. I don't have anything worth stealing and neither does Shelley."

"I don't think that was the point . . ." Donovan began, and then I opened the door and whatever else he had been about to say was silenced by my gasp of disbelief.

I stood in the doorway with my jaw hanging open.

Donovan moved up behind me, looking over my shoulder and saying, "What? What's wrong?" And then he saw, too, and after a startled "Whoa!" he fell silent.

Room 224 at the Quad had been ransacked.

Every drawer was standing open, contents spilling over the edges. Both dressers looked like trash cans after an attack by scavenging dogs.

The closet door yawned open. The shoes and shoeboxes and laundry bags and discarded clothing and fallen hangers and extra purses and piles of sweaters had been flung this way and that, littering the hardwood floor like debris from an explosion.

The drawers on both desks were jutting forward. One of Shelley's had fallen to the floor, its contents scattered around it as if the drawer had suddenly spit everything out in disgust.

My bedside table had been swept clean of papers and pencils, my alarm clock, my hairbrush, and the change I dumped there every night. Shelley's bedside table, too, was clear. The tops of our bookcases, which had earlier been littered with piles of papers and note-books, were completely bare.

The room looked like a violent wind had rushed in through the open window and swept the room from corner to corner and back again, taking with it everything that wasn't nailed down and tossing it to the floor.

And my computer was on. I do not ever, ever leave my computer on when I leave the room for more than a few minutes.

When I had taken it all in, I still didn't move on into the room. I stood in the doorway, my arms hanging at my sides as if they didn't know what to do, my mouth open, my heart spiraling downward to somewhere just above my knees, my spine feeling as if someone were tapping on it with an ice-coated knife.

"Are you okay?" Donovan said from behind me.

"No," I answered softly when I found my voice. "I'm not."

Chapter 4

I don't know how long I stood there, my eyes slowly going over every inch of space in the room until the chaos had sunk in.

Why was my computer on?

I'd forgotten that Donovan was there, until he said, finally, "Looks like you guys could use a good housekeeper." Although his tone was light, I knew he was forcing it. No one could look around that room without being stunned by how very thorough the intruder had been. It looked as if nothing had gone untouched. Nothing.

When I didn't answer Donovan, because I couldn't, he said, grimly this time, "Better call security. Want me to call?"

Finding my voice, I said, "I'll call." My words had a hollow ring to them, as if I were speaking across a huge canyon. "I'll call," I said again, and moved across the room like a zombie, in search of the telephone. I finally found it, hiding beneath the puddle of Shelley's bright red bedspread, which had been ripped off the bed and tossed to the floor.

Security was there in less than five minutes. They poked around and asked all kinds of questions, none of which I could answer, and they shook their heads. But they couldn't tell me what had happened or how it had happened or who had wreaked such havoc. They were just about to leave when Shelley, followed by Cameron Truro, Brynne, and Kirk, arrived. When Shelley came to a full, sudden stop in the doorway, the others all piled up behind her.

No one was more surprised than I was when she shrieked, "Addie, what have you *done*?"

When Shelley shrieked, I saw the two security officers exchange a suspicious glance. I could practically read their minds. Roommates argue, one decides to teach the other a lesson, mess up the room some, happens all the time.

Annoyed, I snapped, "Oh, for pete's sake, Shelley, get real! I didn't do this!"

"Well, then, who did?" she asked, stepping into the room gingerly, as if she expected something nestled in that mess on the floor to bite her in the ankle. Her face was the color of the walls, which were supposed to be white, but needed a fresh coat of paint and were basically a repulsive mushroom-gray. "We don't have anything worth stealing."

"You sure there's nothing missing?" one of the guards asked me for the twelve thousandth time.

"Nothing," I repeated once more.

"Well, then," one officer said, shrugging, and they left.

Disheartened, I shrugged, too. Then I walked over and turned off my computer.

"It's late," I said to Shelley as I turned away from the desk. "Do we really feel like having company?" I sure didn't.

I could tell by the way she whirled around, then motioned all of them inside that she'd forgotten they were with her. "It's Friday night, Addie," she said, flopping down on her stripped bed. "I wasn't ready to go to sleep. But . . ." She glanced slowly around the room, letting the chaos register. "If I'd known . . ."

"How could you have known?" Donovan asked, taking a seat in my desk chair. "Addie was as shocked as you were. Anything like this ever happen before?"

Cameron Truro sat down beside Shelley, which for some reason surprised the heck out of me, and Brynne and Kirk moved over to sit on my bed. I stood in the middle of the room, ankle-deep in papers and books and notebooks and sheets and sweaters and blankets and backpacks and socks.

"No," Shelley and I said in one voice.

"Never," Shelley added.

"It's happened to other people on campus, though," Brynne volunteered. "Last year. I heard about this one girl . . ."

"Never mind!" Kirk said, putting a gentle hand over her mouth. "The last thing they need to hear now is a horror story. Look," he said to me, "maybe it's a good thing we came back here with Shelley. We'll help straighten up this mess. If you two try to do it by yourselves, you'll be up all night. The Games are tomorrow, and you'll be too beat to go. You don't want to miss them, do you?"

The Games. I'd forgotten. I'd been looking forward to the all-day Saturday event, but in the shock of the bus accident and now this disaster in our room, I'd completely forgotten. No surprise there. It was a miracle that I could even remember what day it was, after the things that had happened.

If the weather was good, and it was supposed to be, The Games, a series of athletic events that anyone could take part in, would be held outside, in the stadium. If not, the events would be switched to the new tennis dome. Shelley and I had both signed up. I was running in a relay race, and Shelley and Brynne had teamed up for doubles tennis. I'm not all that athletic, and Shelley's even less so, but it had sounded like fun.

Kirk was right. If Shelley and I put the room back together by ourselves, it would take us forever. Although I wasn't wild about the idea of people I hardly knew handling my things, I still wanted to take part in tomorrow's events. And for that, I needed a decent night's sleep, if that was at all possible now.

"Okay," I agreed, "that'd be good. If you'll all help, we might finish before dawn's early light. Thanks for offering."

"I don't see how we can help," Brynne complained, leaning back against the wall as if she were exhausted. "We don't know where anything goes."

Cameron bent to pick up the edge of Shelley's bedspread. "Bedspread," he said to Brynne. "Bedspread goes on bed." Smiling slightly, he pointed to an upended sneaker on the floor. "Shoe . . . closet." An index finger moved around the room. "Books . . . bookcase. Papers . . . desk," until Brynne finally sighed and said, "Okay, okay, I get the message."

"Are you sure nothing's missing?" Donovan asked as we worked side by side picking up papers and books and clothing.

"I'm sure. At least, so far. Nothing important, anyway. My computer's still here, and Shelley's stereo, and I see my camera over there under my bed."

"Then," Donovan picked up the first two pages of the rough draft of my English paper, "robbery couldn't have been the motive for this invasion."

I took the pages from him. "Excuse me? Motive?"

"Could they have been looking for something?" he asked, depositing a notebook on my desk.

I thought about that for a minute. "Looking for something? Like what? What would anyone be looking for?" I answered incredulously, as if it were the stupidest question I'd ever heard.

It was his turn to think for a minute. I liked the way his mouth was set as he concentrated, and the way his dark eyebrows came together and the way his eyes seemed to deepen in color. "Well, in the movies it's usually microchips or incriminating photographs or stolen money." His eyes moved to mine. "I guess you wouldn't be hiding anything like that, right?"

"I'm not hiding anything at *all*." I was tired and upset and scared, and so I said, raising my voice, "Shel, you hiding any microchips over there?" She gave me a weird look and went on replacing books in her bookcase.

Donovan didn't laugh. Instead, his lips clamped together more tightly and he flushed angrily. "Okay," he said, "I was just trying to help you figure things out." And he left my side to go help Shelley at the bookcase.

I hadn't meant to be so short with him. Or hurt his feelings. But it seemed to me that he'd overreacted. What was I supposed to say? He had suggested that someone was looking for something valuable in a room where there just *wasn't* anything valuable. The idea was ridiculous. I didn't even know what a microchip looked like.

"I just think someone came into the wrong room," I announced as I began replacing clothes on hangers. "That's all. They thought someone else lived here, not Shelley and me."

Donovan ignored my comment. I guessed that meant that if I wasn't going to consider his theory, he wasn't going to pay any attention to mine, either.

"You really think that?" Kirk asked, looking up from the floor where he was gathering together more papers. "That it was just a mistake?"

"Sure." I didn't sound sure. Deliberately

strengthening my voice, I said, "Of course. What else? He thought we were rich, that maybe he'd find something of value here, and boy, was he ever wrong, right, Shelley?"

Shelley didn't answer. She was kneeling beside her bed, her back to me, and she was talking to Cameron Truro in a low voice. He seemed to be hanging onto every word.

I let myself be comforted by my new, sensible theory. Someone had thought we were rich and had come into our room hoping to escape with goodies. We had fooled him. We didn't *have* any goodies.

"He must have been really ticked off when he had to go away empty-handed," I said aloud, forcing a chuckle.

Donovan stood up, wiped his hands on his jeans, pushed a stray clump of hair away from his forehead, and said directly to me, "Are you trying to convince us or yourself?"

Suddenly I was close to tears because although all of us had been at it for what seemed a long time, the room was still pretty much a mess, and because I was tired and still in a state of semishock, and because I wanted, so much, to believe my nice, comforting theory. I stared at Donovan, blinking back the unwanted tears. "What?" I said again.

"Well," he continued doggedly, "your computer is still here, and Shelley's stereo is still here, and that looks like a perfectly good camera under your bed. So he didn't have to leave empty-handed, even if he *had* walked into the wrong room. Unless . . ."

"Unless what?" I snapped, not wanting to hear the answer but knowing that I should.

"Unless he was looking for something in particular in this particular room, and he didn't find it."

And while I was fighting to keep Donovan's theory from entering my brain, where it would settle and insist on being dealt with, Kirk nodded and said, "Which means," bending to deposit one final book in Shelley's bookcase, "that he'll be back."

Chapter 5

Kirk was right. If Donovan's theory was true, the intruder would be *back*. I couldn't deal with that.

So I banished the thought, as effectively as if the words had never been uttered.

When we had cleaned up enough of the mess to clear a path to our beds, everyone left, and Shelley and I collapsed. Her eyes slammed shut the minute her head hit the pillow, but I stayed awake a long time. I couldn't help it. I knew I needed a good night's sleep for The Games the next day. I also knew it wasn't going to happen. If we won the relay race tomorrow, it wouldn't be because of me. I'd be lucky if I had enough strength to get to the finish line.

Images in my head kept me awake. Pictures of a bloody body beneath the bus, pictures of the shambles Donovan and I had walked in on.

Two disasters in one day were enough to keep anyone awake all night.

Lucky Shelley. She'd been as upset as I was by the havoc wreaked in our room. But unlike me, she was able to shut it out of her mind and go to sleep.

Why would someone turn on my computer? If they were checking to see if it worked, why hadn't they stolen it when they'd found out that it worked just fine?

They couldn't have been looking for something *in* the computer, because there wasn't anything there. Only my earlier essays for lit class were on there. I'd already turned those in and been graded, so it wouldn't do anyone any good to steal them.

I rolled over onto my side, facing the wall, and buried my face in my pillow. I couldn't stop thinking about what Kirk had said. Something about the guy coming back because he hadn't found what he wanted?

What did I have that someone wanted?

I didn't have a clue.

I cringed at the thought of someone coming into our room and going through our things. But a tiny little part of me couldn't help feeling just a little bit intrigued by the thought of someone going to so much trouble to get their hands on something of mine.

Stupid way to look at it. But when you've never been envied because you've never been the best at something or owned the best of anything, maybe you think things like that.

My last thought before giving in to sleep completely was that we would have to start locking the door from now on.

I awoke to a sunny Saturday morning with my eyes feeling sandlogged and my head throbbing as if I'd slept on cement. This was not a good sign. I had an athletic event to compete in at eleven o'clock, which gave me exactly two hours to pull myself together.

The chaos of the night before taunted me as I moved about the room, getting dressed. I knew if I kept thinking about that, or about the bus accident, showing up at The Games would be a total waste of time. Instead, I decided to concentrate totally on my race, and then there wouldn't be any room left in my head for thinking about yesterday's disasters.

I had wanted to squeeze in some computer time before leaving the dorm, but with my head feeling like a balloon about to burst, I changed my mind. When Shelley said she was impatient to get going, I decided fresh air was the only thing that was going to clear the cobwebs. I dressed quickly in shorts and a yellow tank top, imprisoned my wild hair in a ponytail, tied the laces of my running shoes together and, carrying the shoes and my purse, followed Shelley out of the room.

At the last minute, I slipped my computer disk out of my purse and thrust it into an empty pizza box underneath my bed. Just in case Kirk was right and the intruder might return. I didn't have any idea what he was looking for, but he wasn't getting my English paper.

We locked the door and pocketed our keys.

Although we would separate later to take part in our individual events, we planned to watch other competitions together until it was time to participate. "Cam's running in the half-mile," Shelley said proudly as we made our way across campus to the stadium.

I glanced over at her. "Cam? Cameron Truro is now Cam to you? When did all of this happen?"

Telltale spots of pink appeared on her round cheeks. "Last night. And *nothing* happened, except that he told me to call him Cam, he said all of his friends call him that, and we're going to the dance tonight."

I stopped walking. "Shelley! Why didn't you tell me last night?" Her first date at Salem University, with *a very* good-looking guy, and she hadn't even told me!

"If you remember," she said drily, tugging

at my sleeve to urge me onward, "we had a few other things on our minds last night. Then when everyone left, all I wanted to do was sleep, okay? Anyway, I'm telling you now."

"So, do you like him? I mean, is he nice?"

"If he wasn't, I wouldn't be going to the dance with him, would I?"

The dance was being held in the rec center to cap off The Games. A popular rock group was playing, and everyone was getting pretty dressed up. I didn't have a date, and had planned to go with Shelley. Maybe I'd just stay home and work on my paper.

For the first time since I'd arrived on campus, the thought of being in the room alone, especially at night, sent a shiver up my spine.

Well, *that* was new. Since when was I afraid of being alone? My sister and her husband led a very active social life, so I'd spent many long evenings alone in the huge old Victorian house our parents had left us. Like all old houses, it was full of noises, creaks and groans and moans, especially when the wind was blowing. But I'd never been the tiniest bit uneasy staying alone. I was always glad when they left and I had the house to myself. Now here I was getting the heebie-jeebies about being alone in my dorm room.

Well, maybe because no one had ever come

into our big, old house in Braddock and gone from room to room, spilling the contents of drawers and desks and bookcases from one corner to the other. I'd felt safe there because I *was* safe.

Couldn't say the same for room 224 at the Quad, could I? Not after last night.

I wasn't supposed to be thinking about that. To get it off my mind, I made Shelley tell me everything she knew about Cameron Truro.

She didn't know that much about him yet. She said he was "nice." That he'd told her he noticed her at the bus stop yesterday and wanted to meet her. That he was an engineering student like Donovan and he didn't have any sisters or brothers and he'd been an athlete in high school. That he had Professor Nardo for English lit, just as she did, which she seemed to take as a "sign."

Shelley had Nardo at ten. I had that class at eight. "So if he's in your class, how come he never asked you out before?" I asked her as we reached the stadium.

"Oh, he's not in my class," she said, shifting her tennis racket from her left shoulder to her right. "He's in yours."

"No, he's not."

"Yeah, he is. He has Nardo at eight, Mondays, Wednesdays, and Fridays, same as you.

Besides, when I told him you were my room-mate, he said you're Nardo's pet." Shelley grinned. "Everyone in there thinks you're a big-deal, hotshot writer."

Cameron Truro was in my lit class? I'd never noticed him. But the class was big, probably close to one hundred students, so many that we were identified by number. I was fifty-six, although now Professor Nardo called me and some of the other students by our last names. I had never heard her say the name "Truro."

He must sit way at the back, I thought. I sit up front. I had never seen him come in or leave, but maybe I just hadn't noticed.

"I know what you're thinking," Shelley said quietly as we surveyed the bleachers to pick out good seats. "You're wondering why some-one who looks like Cameron would ask me out. That's what you're thinking, aren't you?"

Maybe that's why Shelley and I are friends. We both have a serious self-esteem problem. I wasn't surprised that someone had asked Shelley to the dance. What surprised me now wasn't that she'd been asked, it was that she'd actually accepted.

"I wasn't thinking any such thing," I said. "I was thinking that Cameron Truro must be awfully smart to know a good thing when he sees it. That's what I was thinking."

She smiled shyly. We took seats midway up in the bleachers. The stadium was only half-full, but there was a thin, steady stream of latecomers arriving.

By the time I left to begin warming up for the relay race, Donovan, Brynne, and Kirk had joined us, and Shelley told me in an aside that Cam would be joining them after he'd showered. Cam didn't win the half-mile, but he'd come in third. Brynne and Shelley's tennis match wasn't until two. I promised to come and watch, wished Shelley luck, and I left, with Kirk calling after me, "Don't drop the baton, Addie!"

That was, of course, my nightmare. I winced, and behind me, they all laughed.

Very funny.

The temperature warmed up right along with me as I did my stretches, and by the time we were lined up at the start, I was glad I was wearing only a tank top and shorts.

I was the third runner on the team. Linda Carlyle, a sophomore who was a big-deal swimmer, and Tracy Quinn, a fellow freshman, were running the first two legs.

I wasn't that nervous. It wasn't the Olympics. It was just an event put on by the athletic department to drum up interest in sports and give some of us a chance to get acquainted. There weren't any medals or trophies being handed out, and I didn't think the losers would be disgraced.

So I was reasonably relaxed. Still, I wanted to win, especially when Linda almost flew around the track and Tracy did likewise. I could see by the huge stadium clock high up on one wall that our team's time so far was pretty awe-inspiring, and I was determined not to spoil that.

I grabbed that baton from Tracy's extended hand behind me as if it were a gold ring worth millions, and then I was off, legs pumping furiously, concentrating on nothing but the track beneath my feet, remembering my breathing, setting my sights on the finish line where I would pass the baton to "Tiny" Pasquino, the fastest runner on our team.

I ran really well. I had that wonderful, euphoric feeling of flying, feet barely touching the ground, and I could feel my body almost floating around the track. I know I would have stayed well within the time the first two runners had established, maybe even have bettered it, if . . .

I would have run a perfect race *if* an object hadn't come flying out of nowhere.

It didn't hit me. I was moving too fast for anything to hit me.

But it landed on the track directly in front of my flying feet.

All I saw was a big, gray blur that came at me from the left and then slammed to the ground.

There was nothing I could do to avoid it. I was going too fast, it had appeared too suddenly, and my concentration was on running. There was no time for my brain to switch from "run" mode to "avoid" mode.

The tip of my speeding left foot slammed into the object.

There must be a law of physics that says, when a runner's foot slams into a stationary object and the force of that foot doesn't send the stationary object flying out of the way, it's going to be the runner who flies.

Meaning me.

And I knew. I knew the minute the tip of my shoe hit that sudden, unexpected obstacle that this was not going to be good. Not good at all.

Then I shot up into the air like a rocket and I heard this awful, horrified gasp from the crowd surrounding me in the bleachers. I don't think I screamed. I remember wishing desperately that I could think of some way to stop myself from slamming back down onto that hard, hard ground, and I suppose my arms and legs were waving frantically to find a way to do just that.

But it was out of my control. I would have to go back down. Fast. And hard.

Chapter 6

I woke up in the infirmary. In my Twilight-Zonish state of mind, it took me a few minutes to figure out where I was. But the room's walls and ceiling were whiter than ours, the bed was narrower and harder than the one I was used to. I knew I wasn't in my own room and since my head hurt, I guessed infirmary.

Besides, my elbows and knees were on fire, and my head felt like someone was splitting it open with a very sharp axe.

Shelley was standing on one side of my narrow white cot, her face a sickly gray-green. She'd been crying, something she almost never did. There were skinny little tracks of black mascara on her cheeks and she'd bitten off every last trace of lipstick.

Donovan McGarry was standing opposite her. His bushy, dark eyebrows were drawn together in what looked like a worried frown.

"Relax," I told them, reaching up to feel the center of my forehead, which seemed to hurt the most. It was thick with soft white gauze. "I'm alive. I *think*. I hurt too much to be dead." I looked up at Shelley. "I don't have any broken bones, do I?"

She shook her head. "No broken bones. But you messed up your head pretty bad."

I laughed. It hurt. My forehead felt like someone with a very hefty, wooden bat had mistaken it for a baseball. "My head was already messed up pretty bad. Who knows this better than you?"

She did laugh a little then. Very little. Still, her face wasn't quite as green now.

"So," I asked the doctor who came into the room then, "am I scarred for life?" I said it lightly, but the thought had crossed my mind. Judging by the bandage on my forehead, I had slammed into that track face-first.

"No," the middle-aged doctor in the white coat said, "no scars. But you might not want to pose for any pictures for a while" — pointing to my forehead — "until that heals. You scraped off several layers of skin. Probably look pretty scary for a week or two."

I could live with that. And no broken bones. I considered myself lucky.

When the doctor had checked my eyes for

any sign of concussion (and found none, she said), and then my pulse, and given me a pain pill, she left.

I asked Shelley and Donovan what, exactly, I had tripped over.

"A discus," Donovan said first. "A bunch of guys were practicing out in the center of the stadium and apparently one's aim was really off. They all denied tossing it, of course, but one of them had to have let it fly. Where else would it have come from? It settled on the ground right in front of you. There was no way you could avoid it. And you hit it at top speed."

"It's a wonder you didn't break your neck," Shelley said. "The way you flew up into the air and then slammed back down again. We all thought you were . . ." Her voice caught in her throat. "I mean, you were lying there so still, not moving a muscle. It didn't look like you were even breathing."

I settled back against the pillow and asked about The Games.

They answered all of my questions. Shelley hadn't played tennis in The Games, after all. She'd talked someone else into being Brynne's doubles partner so she could follow my stretcher to the infirmary. By the time they got to the part about Brynne claiming to have too weak a stomach to spend more than two seconds in the infirmary, my pill had kicked in and my eyelids felt like they weighed a ton. "I'm not going to grow old in this place, am I?"

"You get out tomorrow," I heard from what seemed to be a great distance. "We'll come to get you."

"What day is this?" I murmured.

"It's still Saturday."

I let the soft, fluffy pink clouds carry me away.

I woke up off and on during the day and later that night, but except for an hour in the evening when Donovan and Shelley brought me something to eat, I slept.

I remember waking up once during the night and wondering why the discus thrower who had accidentally sabotaged my run had lied about it. It wasn't as if he'd done it on purpose. The thing must have flown out of his hand before he was ready to let it go. So why hadn't he just told the truth?

The question made my headache worse. It pounded, thump, thump, thump, as if someone in heavy boots were kicking me right between the eyes. Why . . . thump . . . hadn't the discus thrower . . . thump . . . told . . . thump . . . the truth . . . thump, thump?

I had no idea.

Unless . . . unless it was because the discus

hadn't come from one of the athletes out on the field.

Unless it was because the discus had come from somewhere *else*. Some*one* else.

Why would someone who *wasn't* one of the discus throwers toss a discus in my path as I ran the track? Crazy. A crazy thing to think.

The medication was planting weird ideas in my aching head.

I went back to sleep. I slept until morning.

By the time Kirk, and Donovan, in denim cutoffs and a white T-shirt that read, "IF YOU'RE CLOSE ENOUGH TO READ THIS YOU'RE IN MY WAY," and Shelley, in a pretty, flowered slip dress over a pink short-sleeved T-shirt arrived, I was dressed and ready to go. Anxious to go, in fact. I don't like hospitals, and the infirmary was nothing more than a miniature hospital.

I felt a little self-conscious about the thick, stupid bandage plastered across my forehead, but knew I'd look a lot worse if the bandage *hadn't* been there. I'd seen the wound this morning when the nurse changed the dressing, and it was really gross.

The doctor had said it would heal good as new, and I chose to believe her, since the alternative was too repulsive to even think about.

She had also said I was to "rest" until Tuesday. Which meant no classes for me on Monday.

Shelley vowed to take good care of me. And I had friends to help me out. Donovan certainly seemed to have every intention of becoming a friend. That suited me fine.

I wouldn't just lie around all day Monday. I'd work on my paper. Professor Nardo couldn't fault me for being a day late, since the accident hadn't been my fault.

"Are you guys absolutely sure," I asked as I rather shakily made my way from the infirmary back to the dorm, "that it was one of the discus throwers who sabotaged my run? I mean, I can't figure out why anyone would lie about something like that. It *was* an accident, right? So why not just 'fess up?"

Donovan shrugged. "Probably afraid of the consequences. At the time the athletic director started asking questions, we still didn't know if you were going to be okay. I'm not sure I'd have admitted the truth if I'd been responsible."

"Don't *you* think it was one of the discus throwers?" Shelley asked me. "Who else could it have been?"

"I don't know who it could have been, or why anyone would do something so stupid and dangerous. I just think it's weird that someone would lie about it, that's all." I hadn't planned to say any more, but my lips kept moving and I heard myself saying, "And then there's that business of our room being trashed. Doesn't that seem awfully coincidental? Don't you think the two things might be connected somehow?"

"Our room wasn't trashed, Addie," Shelley disagreed as we reached the Quad. "Trashing means destroying things, spray-painting the walls, stuff like that. Nothing was ruined."

"Nothing was left untouched, either," I said. "Someone came into my room and made a gigantic mess of things, and then someone tossed a discus onto a track when I was running. Don't you think those two things together might mean something?"

"It's *my* room, too," Shelley pointed out. "And nothing's happened to *me*."

"You weren't running the relay," I retorted as we entered our room.

"I'll stay here with you," Shelley said when I was settled in bed, a bag of chips and a cold can of grape soda, my favorite, at my elbow, courtesy of my thoughtful roommate.

I almost nodded and then I remembered how much it hurt to move my head. Instead, I looked over at Shelley. I didn't want to ask her about Cam, in case the date the night before hadn't gone so great. No one had said anything about the dance after The Games. Maybe she'd had a miserable time. So instead, I asked, "Do you have plans tonight?"

"She *could* have plans," Kirk interjected before Shelley could answer. "She cancelled her date with Cam last night because of what happened to you, so he asked her out again for tonight, and she said she'd have to wait and see how you were. I was standing right there when he asked." Kirk and Cam were friends, Shelley had told me.

Shelley had seemed interested in Cameron Truro. "You're not going?" I asked her, trying to frown but finding it impossible. Adhesive tape pinioned my eyebrows in place.

"Of course I'm not going." She plopped down on the bed. "You just got out of the infirmary. I'll go another time."

Kirk said he had to study, told me to rest and get better, and left.

"I'll stay here with Addie," Donovan told Shelley when Kirk had gone. "You go on your date and have fun."

Shelley shook her head stubbornly. "Cameron Truro isn't going to disappear off the face of the earth tonight. And I only have one roommate and best friend. Who's more important?"

Any other time, I would have said, "No one, of course." But this was only Shelley's second invitation from a guy since we'd arrived on campus. And she'd already cancelled one invite. Because of me. There was hope between her and Cameron, and I didn't want to see it disappear.

"Three's a crowd, Shelley," I said, trying to wriggle my eyebrows in a suggestive manner.

She got the message. She looked from me to Donovan and then back again, and this time, her cheeks really got red. "Oh," was all she said. But she jumped up off the bed, grabbed the phone and took it into the bathroom, closing the door. She came out a minute or two later, smiling. "Well, if you're sure," she said, picking up her purse. "I told Cam I'd meet him at the fountain on the Commons at eight. But first, I've got to run to the mall. Can I get you guys anything before I leave?"

"Not a thing." I suppose I was grinning. I don't often get to play Cupid, and never, ever have with Shelley, so I was feeling very pleased with myself.

When the door had closed behind her, Donovan pulled my desk chair over beside the bed and took a seat.

"So," he said, leaning forward slightly and looking directly into my eyes, "why do you think that someone deliberately threw that discus onto the track while you were running?"

I wasn't sure I wanted to discuss this with him. I didn't want him thinking I was paranoid or semihysterical. That didn't seem like a good way to begin a relationship.

Stalling, I said, "I need an aspirin. I think there's some in my purse." I glanced around the room. "The question is, where did I put my purse?"

I watched from my bed as Donovan searched the room first with his eyes, then, finding nothing, got up and moved from chair to desk to dresser, lifting objects, poking around on flat surfaces, opening the closet door and peering inside. Then he moved back to his chair beside my bed again. "I don't see it," he said. "Didn't leave it at the infirmary, did you?"

The thing was, I couldn't remember *having* it at the infirmary. I tried to remember when I'd last seen the purse. Where had I left it when I began my run?

In the bleachers, at Shelley's feet. I hadn't taken it with me down to the track.

"Did Shelley bring my purse to the infirmary?"

Donovan shrugged. "I wouldn't remember something like that. Want me to call over there and check?"

"Good idea. My student ID's in there, and my driver's license, and I just cashed this month's check from my sister. But," I added, "at least I'd already taken the disk out."

"Disk?"

"My lit paper. I was carrying the disk around in my purse, but didn't want it lying around in the hot sun while I ran, so I put it somewhere else."

"Your purse is probably at the infirmary," Donovan said, and reached for the phone to dial. He hung up the phone and shook his head negatively.

The purse wasn't there.

Chapter 7

I was so sure that Shelley wouldn't have forgotten my purse, I asked Donovan to search the room thoroughly. When Kirk returned with Brynne, we put them to work, too. "Didn't we just clean this place up?" Brynne complained as they overturned pillows and clothing and piles of books, looking for the missing shoulder bag.

They didn't find my purse.

"I need it," I said, lying back against the pillow because my head was aching again. "I need my license and my ID, and my sister's going to have a fit about that money if I don't get it back."

"All I know is," Brynne said, signalling to Kirk to join her, "Shelley didn't have your purse when she was running along beside your stretcher when you left the stadium. She only had one purse, her own. That ratty old denim thing. I would have noticed if she'd had two purses on her shoulders, Addie."

"She wouldn't have just left my purse in the bleachers, Brynne."

"She was freaked by what happened to you. We all were. The minute you landed, we were out of those bleachers like a shot and running down to the track. Shelley had her own purse on her shoulder. But yours was probably lying at her feet, right?"

"Right."

"Well, she wouldn't have remembered that. She was too frantic. Your purse is probably still there, unless one of the custodians picked it up. Maybe it's at lost and found."

"Or maybe it's still in the bleachers," I said crankily. "Want us to go hunt for it?" Kirk offered. Obviously I was in no condition to be climbing on bleachers.

"That'd be great." I described, as well as I could remember, where Shelley and I had been sitting.

"They'll find it," Donovan said when they had gone. "If it's not at the stadium, it'll be at lost and found."

Maybe. Even if someone had stolen it, once they'd taken the money, wouldn't they dump the purse? And then someone else would find it and turn it in to lost and found or, since my driver's license and student ID were in my wallet, bring it to the Quad and give it to the girl at the lobby desk.

I could only hope that Donovan was right, that Kirk and Brynne wouldn't return empty-handed.

Shelley returned before they did. She triumphantly held up a large bag from one of the boutiques in the mall. "Found the perfect blouse," she said happily, pulling her purchase free of its wrapping and holding up a silky, red, long-sleeved blouse.

"I thought you were broke. Is that silk? You didn't buy that in a discount store."

Shelley laughed. "Discount? Cam Truro is not a discount-clothing kind of person, Addie."

"No, but *you* are. At least, you were. That must have cost a fortune, Shelley. You didn't even have enough money for a hot dog yesterday."

Annoyance flashed across her face as she hung the blouse on a hanger. "I had money. I just forgot to bring it to the stadium with me. Lighten up, okay? This is a very special occasion, Addie. I can't wear just any old thing." When she turned away from the closet, the annoyed expression had been replaced by one of concern. "How are you feeling? Head still ache?"

"I'm okay." Not. "But my purse is missing. Do you remember what you did with it yesterday?"

She looked blank. "Your purse?"

"My purse. You kept it for me, remember? In the bleachers?"

"Your purse?" she repeated.

"Yeah, Shelley, you know, the big, brown thing with the wide strap that I carry on my shoulder everywhere I go? You said you'd keep an eye on it while I ran yesterday. But it's not here and it's not at the infirmary. Brynne said you ran from the bleachers when I fell. Did you forget to grab my purse?"

Her face cleared then. "Oh, Addie, I'm sorry! I guess I did. I don't remember reaching down to pick it up. I was so panicked, I forgot it was there. Did you have much money in it?"

"This month's allowance." And if I didn't get it back, which I really didn't expect to, I'd have to call Mary and ask for another check and she'd wail, "Oh, Addie, honestly, can't you keep track of anything? Money doesn't grow on trees, you know."

No one in this world knew better than I did that money did *not* grow on trees. I'd heard that phrase so often, it was practically my theme song. One reason I cared so much about my grades in college was, I couldn't wait to begin supporting myself. I hated having to be dependent on Mary and Stokes. Some of the insurance money that our parents had left us was mine, but I never knew exactly how much there was. I knew that part of it had been used to buy Esmerelda, my car, and later, my computer. Mary had given me the impression that there wasn't much left after that, which was why they had to help out. I hated that.

Shelley was still apologizing for forgetting my purse when Kirk and Brynne returned, their cheeks red from the sun blazing down on them while they searched the bleachers. They were empty-handed.

But instead of saying, "Sorry, Addie, no luck," and taking seats in the room, they stood just inside the doorway, hesitating.

"You didn't find it, I take it," I said. "And I guess lost and found, in the administration building, is closed on Sunday, right?"

"Addie," Kirk said, and stopped. He glanced at Brynne helplessly, and she shrugged and looked at me.

"What?" I sat up. "What's wrong?"

"We went past your car on the way back," Brynne said. "In the parking lot."

"Esmerelda? What about her?" I knew, with a fluttering of my heart, that this was not going to be good news.

"Someone broke in and . . ." Kirk said regretfully. "It's kind of a mess."

I was out of that bed as if I'd been shot from it, and down the hall and down the stairs to the lobby, everyone else rushing after me.

"You shouldn't be running like that, Addie," Shelley called.

I ignored her.

"Whatever happened to Essie," she yelled after me, "it's not worth another trip to the infirmary!"

They caught up with me outside. I slowed down then to a fast walk toward the parking lot.

"When we passed the car," Brynne continued as we neared the parking lot, "I could tell that there was something weird about it. So we went over and when we got close enough, we could see that the door handle was broken, almost broken right off, Addie, and then we looked inside . . ."

We were at the car then, and Brynne stopped talking. From the outside, the only evidence that anything was wrong with Essie was the chrome door handle, hanging limply like a broken limb. The yellow paint around the handle was gone, the hand-painted daisies scraped away, revealing bare metal. Rage swept over me, making me dizzy.

With the lock broken, I didn't need a key to get into the car. I pulled the door open gingerly, carefully, half-expecting it to fall off in my hands. Then I stood there on the asphalt, leaning against the open door for support while I stared with bleak eyes at the damage to the interior of my car.

The glove compartment was hanging open. Its contents — maps, a package of cheese-and-peanut-butter crackers, two rolls of breath mints, a notepad, a pen, the registration, two overdue library book notices, my proof of insurance and a map of Twin Falls, Salem's host community — were scattered about on the worn, ragged gray carpet. The carpet itself had been torn free and was wedged sideways beneath the compartment, its edges curling loosely, and the books that had been piled on the front seat had been tossed into the back seat.

But that wasn't all. The vinyl upholstery covering the front seat, an ugly brown tweed, had been slit open from the top of the driver's seat to the bottom. There was yellowed stuffing everywhere, huge puffs of it on the floor and on the seat and clinging to the steering wheel, like pieces of a frizzy blonde wig. The passenger's side of the seat had been shredded in the same way.

The sun beating down on the top of my head in the open parking lot intensified my headache. Or maybe it was the destruction facing me that made my skull pound.

Behind me, Shelley said softly, "Oh, Addie." Donovan muttered an oath under his breath. Brynne murmured, "What a disgusting mess!" and Kirk said, "I don't believe this."

I believed it. I wouldn't have if someone had told me about it. If someone had come running up to my room and shouted, "Addie, your car's been broken into and the carpet's been ripped up and the stuffing's out of the upholstery and it just looks so terrible!" I would have thought they were kidding around, and probably would have laughed and said, "Yeah, right."

I wasn't laughing now. Actually, I was crying. Because I had to believe what I was seeing with my own eyes. How could I pretend it wasn't real?

It was too much. It was just all too much. First our room had been invaded, then the discus had been tossed onto the track and I'd ended up in the infirmary, and I couldn't find my purse and my money was probably gone and Mary was going to be really pissed, and now this!

I knew perfectly well that I had to take care of myself. I'd known that for a long time. I didn't tell other people my troubles (except Shelley) and I tried not to whine when things weren't going right. I figured, since what I was shooting for was to be pretty much responsible for myself, I had to learn to handle the bad things by myself instead of dumping them on other people's shoulders.

But there had been too many bad things, suddenly and without warning, and they'd all happened too fast. And this one was different. This was awful, horrible. It was mean and cruel, and it had caught me off guard.

That's why I let go of the door, sank down on the ruined front seat of my car on the passenger's side, put my face in my hands even though there were people standing right there in front of me, and just went ahead and cried.

And I didn't care what they thought.

· Chapter 8

When Brynne silently handed me a packet of tissues, I took it gratefully and wiped my eyes and nose. Then I got out of the car and shut the passenger's side door. The broken handle clanked against the door as it closed, as if reminding me that it, too, was hurting.

"So," I asked of no one in particular, "who do I take Esmerelda to? Who can put her back together?"

"There's a guy in town," Donovan answered quickly, clearly relieved that I'd pulled myself together. "He's good, and he won't steal you blind. I'll give him a call if you want."

If Mary and Stokes wouldn't pay for Esmerelda's repairs, I'd get a job. I would have applied for one sooner, but I'd been afraid it would affect my grades, so I held off. Now I might not have any choice. I wasn't going to leave poor Essie as she was. She was a good pal, and she didn't deserve to be abandoned now just because someone had taken a knife to her.

A very sharp knife, judging by the destruction. I shuddered. The image of someone armed with a sharp knife slashing the upholstery in my beloved car made my stomach churn. What if I'd been in the car when he attacked it? Would I, too, have been shredded?

Even if I'd had my keys, it would have been pointless to lock three of the car doors when one was so obviously broken. We went back to the room, I called security, and they said they would send someone over. Then I called the garage in town.

A very nice man answered, was very sympathetic, and said he'd send someone to pick it up.

No one had said, "Why would someone do such a rotten thing?"

No one had asked me who I thought had done it.

No one had said, "Aren't you scared, Addie?"

Yes. I was scared. Very scared.

I plopped down on my bed, grateful to be sitting. My knees felt watery.

"Your head's been bleeding again," Brynne said. "I can see red through the bandage." The tone of her voice was disapproving, as if I'd deliberately smeared blood on my forehead just to offend her.

"You shouldn't have been running," Kirk said. He was sitting on the floor beside Brynne, his back against Shelley's bed. "You're as white as the wall. Maybe we should call a doctor or something."

"No doctor," I said firmly. Suddenly, I wanted nothing more than to get rid of them. All of them. They were sitting there as if they expected to stay a while. But I needed to be alone. There was something very, very wrong in my life, and I couldn't think about that with people staring at me as if they expected me to collapse at any moment.

"You can stay to talk to the security people," I said, "and tell them what you saw. But then you have to go away. I need to sleep," I added, lying down on the bed to make my point. "I just need to sleep."

"Shelley's going out," Donovan reminded me. "You don't want to be here alone, do you? Maybe that's not such a good idea."

That was when I realized how scared I really was. Because I immediately thought, *Maybe*? Someone had been angry enough with me to take a knife to my car and Donovan thought *maybe* I shouldn't be alone?

I was really terrified. An intruder in our

room hadn't done it, because nothing had been destroyed and so it hadn't seemed so terrible. Tripping over the discus hadn't done it because that could have been an accident. And I still hoped that my purse was simply lying around the stadium somewhere.

But now my car had been viciously ravaged. Everyone knew whose car that was. Thanks to my amateurish artwork, there wasn't another one like it on campus. Even if there had been, my license plate read, simply, ADAIR, a gift from Stokes and Mary.

The person who had attacked Esmerelda had to know exactly who she belonged to.

So hearing Donovan tell me that maybe I shouldn't be alone on this particular Sunday night chilled me to the bone.

But instead I said, in the calm, rational voice of a person who feels secure and safe, "Shelley isn't going out for hours yet. She'll spend all afternoon getting ready. By the time she leaves, I'll be sound asleep. I won't even know she's gone. And she'll lock the door when she leaves."

They seemed to buy that. If anyone heard the trembling underneath my calm, rational voice, they didn't let on.

The security people came then, a tall, skinny guy and a middle-aged woman, both in uniform.

They asked questions. I told them exactly where Esmerelda was and they left, telling all of us to stay where we were. They were back in half an hour to ask more questions, making notes on small white pads as we struggled to answer.

But none of us knew anything. Except that someone suddenly didn't like me very much. We just didn't know why.

After they left, I said into the sudden silence, "Would you guys mind going now, too? I hate to be rude, but I really have to sleep. I'll think about all of this later, when I wake up. And we'll talk about it then, okay?"

Brynne looked relieved, but Donovan's face filled with doubt. Before he could repeat his earlier warning, I said quickly, "I'll call you later, okay? I promise. But right now, my head is really hurting."

When they were leaving, and Donovan was standing in the doorway, he turned back to say, "You're not going to work tonight, are you? You said you had a lit paper to do. You're not going to try and finish that tonight?"

"No. I have an extra day now, since I won't be going to class tomorrow. And I'll feel more like working after I've had a good night's sleep."

Finally they left, closing the door gently behind them.

Being reminded of the lit paper set the tiny little wheels in my tiny little brain in motion. I'd told Donovan the truth. I hadn't planned to work on the assignment, not after the kind of day I'd had. And I did have all day tomorrow to work on it.

But something about that essay was nagging at me . . .

Shelley came out of the bathroom then. She looked beautiful. The red brought out the color in her cheeks, and she had curled her short, dark hair softly around her face.

"You're wearing makeup," I said in awe. Not since the accountant had absconded with her mother had a powder puff so much as touched her cheek. "You must really like this guy."

"I don't know if I do or not," she said, a bit defensively.

Yeah, right. "Well, anyway, you look gorgeous. He'll fall at your feet and pledge his undying love and loyalty."

Shelley laughed nervously. "I don't *think* so. I'd settle for just having a good time. I feel bad about making him miss the dance last night."

"How do you know he didn't go without you?" I asked.

"I asked someone. He wasn't there." She

frowned as she fastened tiny red earrings in her earlobes in front of the dresser mirror. "The girl I asked wanted to know why *I* wanted to know and I told her that he'd asked me to go with him, but I'd had to cancel. I could tell she didn't believe me. Cameron Truro? Asking someone like me for a date? Never happen, that's what I saw in her face."

"Oh, forget her. He *did* ask you, and then he asked you out again, so what does it matter what she thinks?"

I don't think it sank in. She was still frowning a little when Cam came to pick her up. He really was gorgeous.

He seemed friendly, too. He asked about my computer. I admitted my lack of knowledge, and he said he'd be happy to fill me in on some of the other features of my machine if I wanted. I couldn't tell if he meant it or if he was just trying to impress Shelley's roommate, but I said I'd let him know if I got stumped and needed expert help.

The second the door closed, I was out of that bed and in my desk chair and had the computer switched on.

The thing was, there was no reason for anyone on campus to be angry with me. So the intruder in our room, the discus on the track, the missing purse, and my vandalized Esmerelda couldn't possibly have anything to do with me being a jerk and offending someone.

But there had to be a reason why someone was doing these things.

What if it wasn't because my personality set their teeth on edge? What if it had nothing to do with me at all? Maybe Donovan had been right. What if, instead of deliberately destroying the inside of my car out of rage, the attacker had been simply *looking* for something? Wasn't that really how our room and then my car had looked? As if someone had been tossing the contents left and right in a frantic search?

It was hard to imagine anyone thinking something had been hidden within the upholstery of a car. How would you do that, anyway? Slice a hole in the seat and then sew it back up after you'd hidden whatever in there? Maybe the guy had simply exploded in rage when he hadn't found what he was looking for.

Now there was a scary thought. If he got *that* angry, that easily, and if he was armed with a knife, he wasn't someone I wanted to meet in a dark alley. Or anywhere else, for that matter.

Every time I asked myself what someone could have been looking for, I kept coming up blank, because I couldn't think of anything I had anyone would want. What did I have in my possession that I hadn't had two days ago?

The answer I finally came up with was, my lit paper disk.

I have never received anything less than an A in English. Other subjects, I admit to C's and D's in, even an F in geometry once. But always an A in English. And I was doing especially well in English at Salem. Each time Professor Nardo returned an essay to me, she said, "Congratulations, Adair," and flourished the paper in such a way that most of the people in the class could easily see the bright red "A."

Everyone in there had to know that I was doing very well. They also knew that I wrote my papers on a computer. Nardo had asked how many did, and I'd raised my hand.

I'd heard about cheating on campus. And I'd also heard that some people used computers to cheat, by breaking into a professor's system and stealing an exam. I had no idea how that was done. All I could manage so far on the computer was the word processing program.

There might be someone in English class who saw my new paper as a guaranteed A. Maybe he or she had a guaranteed F, and was desperate to change it any way they could. One too many F's, and there went your college career. Maybe someone was trying to find my disk, use my essay, steal my A, and I would never know. How could I? We never saw each other's papers.

If I hadn't known how really competitive some people can be academically, I'd have thought my theory was ridiculous. But it was the only thing I could come up with that made some sense.

I'd worked hard on this essay. And someone was trying to steal it and claim my work as their own? Is that what it could be? Was someone that desperate for a good grade?

That was *not* going to happen.

Rejoicing that I'd taken the disk out of my purse, I unearthed it from its new home in the empty pizza box under my bed. I slid the disk into the drive, my eyes on the screen anticipating my own, hard-won words.

They weren't there.

There was no title, "Analysis of Charles Dickens's *A Tale of Two Cities*."

There was no byline, "By Adelaide Adair."

There was no heading, "Eng Lit I, MWF, 8:00 A.M., Professor Nardo."

What I was staring at on the screen was not my lit paper.

The disk in the drive wasn't mine.

Chapter 9

What I was looking at on my computer screen as I put a hand to my bandaged head in confusion was a bunch of initials followed by gibberish that meant nothing to me.

I peered more closely at it.

DMJ: CRD. SHBAX. NIXQSSKD.

RLP: MWRAX. MNT MN BLD.

CAY: DD. NIXQSSKD.

MC: NHSS. FKSCD. NT. FIN.

It made no sense. But then I guessed that it wasn't supposed to. Not to anyone other than its author, anyway.

Was the code's author named REDD? Or, REDD could be what he was calling the file, and his name could be something entirely different.

I stared at the screen for a long time, but I didn't come up with any answers.

Then I turned it off, took two aspirin, and went to bed.

Two minutes later, I got back out of bed, removed the disk, and returned it to the pizza box under my bed before crawling back in under the sheet.

I lay awake for what seemed like hours.

I remembered finding the disk in the computer at the library, I remembered my purse slipping off the chair and me bending to pick it up, and I remembered Shelley scaring two years off my life by slipping up on me suddenly. I'd almost fallen, and I'd dropped my own disk into that jumble of newspapers and research materials on the desk.

When I'd recovered, I must have picked up the wrong disk.

So where was mine?

There went my theory about someone trying to steal my lit paper. It wasn't my essay he was looking for, it was his own disk.

So what was the problem? Mine was clearly labelled with my name. Why hadn't he just brought mine to me and asked for his own? I didn't know what *his* name was. Even if the name didn't mean anything to him, he could go to administration and find out where I roomed.

Why hadn't he done that? Why all these nasty, sneaky attempts to retrieve his disk instead of just coming to me and asking for it?

I didn't know. What I did know was that my head was thump-thumping again and I was supposed to be resting and I couldn't work on my paper now, anyway, not without my disk. My Monday off would be wasted unless my disk was returned to me, and I'd be late with a paper for the first time since I'd started classes. Unless the bandage across my forehead brought sympathy from Professor Nardo, which didn't seem likely, there went my A in lit.

What had I accomplished by figuring out all this stuff? It didn't do me any good. And remembering the slicing and dicing done to Esmerelda, I was still as frightened as ever.

Depressed, exhausted, and very confused, I finally fell asleep.

Shelley was all smiles the next morning when I woke up and found her rushing around the room getting ready for class. "I'm meeting Cam for breakfast in the dining hall," she said. "Can I get you anything before I leave?"

"No, thanks. So, I guess you guys hit it off last night," I said.

Shelley whirled, smiled, and fastened her grandmother's locket around the collar of her white shirt. "You could say that. He's really nice, Addie. Smart, too. He knows all about computers and the information highway and all of that new technology stuff."

"You look . . . different this morning."

It was true. Ever since her mother left, Shelley had had this downturn to her lips that made her look sullen, even a little angry. I'd always thought it kept people who didn't know her from approaching her. That look was gone now. She looked happier. And definitely approachable.

I didn't know if I liked Cam Truro or not. I hardly knew him. But if he could do that for Shelley in just one date, he was probably okay.

"You should have seen the look on all those faces when we walked into the theater," she said gleefully as she gave her thick, dark hair a few whacks with a brush. "We got there early, so the lights were still on. You know Marta Gower? The tall blonde who dates only *the* cutest guys on campus? Her jaw almost fell to the floor when she saw me with Cam." Shelley laughed with delight. "And her friends leaned so far forward to see what she was looking at, I thought they'd tumble out of their seats." She dropped the brush onto the dresser and turned around. Her dark eyes were shining. "They just couldn't believe that Cam Truro was with *me*, dumpy old Shelley Karlsen!"

"You're not dumpy." When was she going to

get over that? "You're gorgeous. And could you do me a quick favor before you leave for the halls of ivy? Could you run downstairs and see if someone brought my purse to the lobby? It had my ID in it, so maybe some kindhearted soul found it and delivered it."

"I'll just call the desk. It's almost nine. There should be someone on duty down there. Then, if it's there, I'll get it for you." She dialed on the portable phone, spoke to someone, and hung up.

"So?" I said.

Shelley gave me the bad news, adding, "But you're not going to replace your driver's license today, are you? The doctor said you should rest. Wait until tomorrow and I'll go with you. I don't have a class on Tuesday until two. You can't drive, anyway. You don't have keys for Essie. You'd have to take the shuttle bus."

We both shivered at mention of the bus. "Did you ever find out that guy's name?" I asked her.

"Potsy something."

"You're kidding! His name was Potsy?"

"That's what Cam said. He didn't know the last name, but he said someone told him the guy's nickname was Potsy."

Had to be a high school nickname. People in college didn't have names like "Potsy." I remembered his face for a moment, and that day at the shuttle stop . . . I shook my head to block out the thought.

"Tell Cam I might pick his brain about computers sometime," I said, rolling over and closing my eyes. Maybe he could figure out why mine had been on when I wasn't even in the room.

"Okay. He wants to get to know you, he said. He said he wants to know all of my friends, but especially my roomie and the person who knows me best. Wanted to come up last night, but I told him you'd be asleep. Maybe later today, if you're feeling better. Now," she wagged a stern finger at me, "promise me you're not going to go hunting for your purse or go to the DMV, okay? Wait till tomorrow. You'll be feeling better, and I can go with you."

I wasn't going anywhere. I had no car to drive, and anyway, I had suddenly remembered my confusion from the night before. My stomach rolled over as I realized it might not be safe out there. Not if someone armed with a sharp knife was mad at me. "If you have time, Shelley, maybe you could check out lost and found at Butler Hall for me. Just in case someone turned in my purse."

"I'll try. Take it easy now. Don't get out of

bed unless you absolutely have to. You're not going to work on your essay, are you?"

"I don't know yet. Why?"

"You're supposed to be resting, not sitting in a chair. I'll come back and check on you later."

When she had gone, I rolled over and went back to sleep again, telling myself that when I called lost and found later, my purse would be there. And then I went right on fantasizing. Someone would come knocking on my door to trade disks. I'd give him or her the disk I had, he or she would give me mine, and everything would be fine again. I wouldn't have to go to the DMV. I wouldn't have to call Mary and listen to a lecture about being "responsible" and "keeping track" of things, especially money. I could finish my paper and hand it in on time and my grade would still be a solid A.

Then security would come to tell me they'd caught the person who had trashed my car. He'd thought it was someone else's, the officers would tell me. The vandal hadn't had anything against me at all, didn't even know who I was. He'd just made a mistake.

That scenario was so much better than the one from last night that I hugged it to me like a soft teddy bear and went back to sleep.

Suddenly the loud, annoying roar of a power lawn mower outside, below my window, woke me from a sound sleep.

I couldn't believe it when I glanced at my alarm clock. Noon! I really must have been zonked out.

Only one window was open, cracked no more than an inch or so. I threw the covers aside and stumbled over to get more air into the room, wincing as a very warm sun hit my face and temporarily blinded me.

The fresh air felt wonderful. My T-shirt was clinging to me, damp with perspiration from having too many blankets on as the room warmed up. I leaned out of the window to cool off.

My headache was finally gone.

Salem's campus is beautiful. The buildings are a mix of old and new, some white stone, some brick entwined with ivy, and the grounds are gorgeous, planted with huge, old trees and thick shrubbery and now, rust and yellow and white fall flowers in beds scattered across the rolling green lawns. It was so warm, a few people were lying on blankets on the Commons. I could see them directly beneath my window, on the velvety green square.

The mower that awakened me, a huge monstrosity of black and yellow, sat idling off to one side. No one was sitting on it, but I saw a maintenance man a few feet away, clipping a bush with a pair of giant orange scissors.

I decided it was too gorgeous a day to spend inside, after all. Maybe I'd just take a few minutes to stroll over to the administration building and check out lost and found for my purse.

Then I remembered that no matter how beautiful the campus might look, it wasn't safe out there. Not for me.

On the other hand, this room had been invaded. So how safe was I in *here*?

Because I wanted so much to go outside, I left the window to change into denim cutoffs and a blue T-shirt, then returned to the window to brush my hair up into a ponytail. Might as well soak up as much fresh air as possible. Like the aspirin, it seemed to be making me feel better.

A class must have been dismissed while I was getting dressed, because the lawns below me were more crowded now. I saw Shelley walking by the fountain in the center of the Commons, and I wondered if she knew Cameron Truro was headed her way, coming from the other direction. And there was Donovan, loping along, books in hand, a light breeze blowing his hair, and on another walkway, Brynne, who looked very much as if she were hurrying to catch up with Kirk, some distance ahead of her, his head down. If any of them was calling to anyone else, their voices were lost to the loud grumbling of the mower, and no one turned around to see who was calling.

They all seemed lost in their own little worlds.

A sudden movement behind one of the people sunbathing on the grass caught my eye. I turned my head to look.

The huge power mower was moving forward, very slowly.

But there was no one sitting on the black padded seat.

At first, I thought it was an optical illusion, caused by the sun glaring down into my eyes. The mower *couldn't* be moving.

But as I leaned further out the window, I saw that it was no illusion. Slowly, but purposely, the mower was moving, as if it had just realized it had more grass to mow and it had to do it right this very minute.

It was headed straight toward one of the sun worshippers lying on the Commons.

Chapter 10

I looked for the maintenance man. He was on the far side of the tall, thick bushes now. I could see only a thatch of white hair, the glint of his sunglasses, and a small patch of his red overalls. Behind that thick barrier of leaves and limbs, there was no way he could see that his mower was leaving without him.

I shouted at him from the window. But the mower ran right over my voice, drowning it out.

I looked down again. The one sunbather who lay directly in the path of the mower was a guy I knew only slightly. He was in my earth science class. His name was Bob something. He was alone now, lying on the gray blanket on his stomach, wearing only yellow shorts and earphones, a portable CD player at his side.

I waited for him to hear the mower. I waited for him to lift his head, turn to see what that horrendous noise was, and jump up out of the way.

But the earphones were shutting out every sound except the music on his CD.

I leaned farther out of the window, my hands clutching the sill to keep me from tumbling two floors down. I shouted a warning to Bob. When he didn't hear me, I shouted again, and again, and again. No one noticed. I shouted, screamed, pounded on the wooden window frame. I waved one arm frantically, needing the other to maintain my grip on the sill.

There were people down there. Why didn't they look up? If they couldn't hear me over the roar of the mower, why didn't one of them at least notice the huge, lumbering machine relentlessly making its way toward the unsuspecting Bob?

Finally, someone did. Donovan. I saw him glance up and spy me in the window. At first he must have thought I was waving at him, because he smiled and waved back. But when I gestured wildly toward the mower and pointed frantically at Bob, Donovan understood that my arms weren't flailing in a friendly greeting.

He turned then, and his eyes followed my pointing finger. I saw him stare for a moment as if he, like me, couldn't believe what he was seeing.

Then I saw his mouth open. I could almost see the cry that floated uselessly out into the air in the direction of the unaware sun worshipper, who still lay quietly, listening to music, his eyes on an open book settled on the blanket beneath him.

Donovan must have shouted at Kirk then, walking on the path opposite him, because I saw Kirk break into a run. A second later, Shelley picked up on the fact that something was going on, and she ran, too, toward Kirk. Then all three were racing toward the runaway mower.

Too late.

Although I was still screaming and shouting and pounding on the window frame in a near-hysterical frenzy, desperate to get Bob's attention, the mower hadn't had that much ground to cover to get to him.

Donovan, Shelley, and Kirk, and now Brynne and Cam, were racing, their arms waving, their mouths open in shouts of alarm. But they were only halfway to the gray blanket when the mower reached its edge.

Bob must have sensed something then, some vibration on the ground behind him, some noise, something out of the ordinary. Because he did turn his head then, did glance over his shoulder.

I saw his eyes widen in horror, saw the muscles in his back tense visibly, thought I saw him cry out in terror.

Above him, I was screaming at him to roll out of the way, roll out of the *way*, hurry, hurry, there's still time . . .

He did roll out of the way.

Just as the mower bore down upon him, he threw himself sideways, off the blanket.

But he was not . . . quite . . . fast . . . enough.

Donovan, Shelley, Kirk, Cam, and Brynne came to a sudden halt on the walkway, knowing there was nothing more they could do.

Later, school administration officials told the campus radio reporter that the "accident victim was a very lucky young man."

Well, maybe. It's true that he could have been killed.

Because he had rolled aside, the blades only caught and sliced off all but one toe on his left foot and two on his right foot.

Bob was alive. But he wouldn't be walking any time soon. Or playing basketball. Not now. Maybe not ever.

I can still hear his scream. It was high and shrill and sounded clearly over the roar of the mower. And it was filled with agony. For many days and nights to come, I would see him writhing in pain on the velvety green grass of the Commons. I would see his face go gray with shock and his eyes, which seemed to be looking directly up at me, go blank. I would see these things over and over again, awake and in dreams that left me weak, sweaty, and shaken.

But my nightmares could never be as horrifying as his.

It was Cam who jumped aboard the mower then, backed it off Bob's mutilated feet, and switched off the engine.

By the time the beastly roar finally died, Bob had stopped screaming. The Commons filled with a deathly, stunned silence.

Gasping for breath, my throat raw from shouting, I sagged against the window frame, my eyes fixated on the eerie scene below me.

Chapter 11

I stood frozen at the window, as if I'd been nailed to the frame. I wanted to race downstairs, join the others on the Commons, see if I could help, but my body wouldn't move.

Even from the second floor, I could see with mind-numbing detail that there was blood everywhere. Dark puddles of it spread across the green velvet lawn.

Bob had stopped screaming. His eyes were open, but he wasn't making a sound.

Other people were. Many among the crowd that had gathered were screaming or crying. I understood that, because I could see how much worse this was than the shuttle bus disaster.

That made no sense. How could it be worse? Someone had *died* at the bus stop, but Bob was still alive. No one was dead here. Why did this seem so much more horrifying?

It's *not* worse, I told myself sternly, it's just messier. So it *looks* worse.

Then I turned away from the window and went downstairs and outside to see for myself just how much worse it really was.

It *was* horrible. And it was chaotic. People who didn't seem to know what to do were running around shouting. Some people left, looking sick, while others arrived to learn the gory details.

People in white medical jackets had been called from the infirmary and were kneeling by Bob's side, bandaging his mutilated foot to stop the flow of blood. They hadn't finished when I got there. I could see what that mower had done to him.

The elderly maintenance man responsible for the huge machine stood off to one side, the expression on his face identical to the one I'd seen on the face of the shuttle bus driver. He repeatedly denied, in a loud voice, that he was responsible. "Just left it for a minute," he insisted. "Stupid thing shouldn't have slipped out of gear like that. Defective, that's what it is, defective."

A security guard came then and led the man away. He'd be blamed for the accident, I knew. Lose his job, maybe even be fined or something. Bob's parents might sue him. He should never have left that mower's engine on and walked away from it, even if it was just a few feet.

"We all shouted at Bob," Donovan told me, his voice hushed with shock, as the victim was loaded on a stretcher and taken away in an ambulance. He was standing off to one side, alone. "But he had those headphones on. Didn't hear a thing until it was too late." He glanced down at me. "You must have seen the whole thing from where you were."

"I did." My own voice was husky, my throat raw. "I screamed my lungs out, but you were the only one who saw me up there."

Someone from security took the runaway lawn mower away to check it out, commenting that it must have "slipped its gears," and people from the landscaping crew quickly went to work cleaning up evidence of the accident. They hosed away the blood, then brought another mower in to even out the grass surrounding the wide swath sliced away by the marauding machine.

Shelley was suddenly at my elbow. Brynne, Kirk, and Cam arrived one at a time, saying they'd been hunting for us in the crowd. They all looked as shaken as I felt.

The new mowing machine was only a few

feet away from us when I noticed something shiny sticking out of the ground. The mower was about to run over it and drive it into the ground. Could be something of Bob's. A watch or ring, maybe. I decided that he had lost enough already and ran to save whatever it was that he might have left behind.

I reached down and scooped it up. Held it in my hand. Looked down at it.

It wasn't Bob's. It was Shelley's. It was the locket her grandmother had given her.

"Shelley?" I held out my hand, palm up, the locket resting inside. "Isn't this yours?"

She'd been talking to Cam. She looked up when I said her name, and her eyes went to my outstretched palm. Surprise registered in her face. One hand went to her throat. "How did that get there?"

"Must have fallen off when you were running over here," Cam suggested. "Is the chain broken?"

The chain wasn't broken. Unfastened, but not broken.

"It does that sometimes," Shelley said, taking the locket from me. "I should have the clasp fixed. I didn't even notice that it was missing. Thanks for grabbing it, Addie. Another minute and it would have been pulverized."

We all began walking away, back toward the

Quad. "The maintenance man will probably be fired," Kirk said. "He kept saying it wasn't his fault."

"Of course he said it wasn't his fault. He'd be too scared to admit the truth. Just like the discus guys on the track, right, Addie?"

Cynical Shelley. Cam hadn't completely transformed her after all. She was still suspicious of people's actions and motives.

"Especially after he saw what had happened to Bob Printz," she added.

"Printz? Is that Bob's last name?" I asked her.

She nodded. "Bob Printz." She glanced over at me. "Don't you remember him from high school?"

"Our high school? He went to Wickley?"

Shelley nodded. "Sure. Big-deal basketball player. You never went to the games, but I went to one or two. Bob Printz is pretty good."

"Was," Donovan reminded her in a low voice. "*Was* a big-deal basketball player."

I didn't remember anyone named Bob Printz. But then, Shelley and I had gone to a huge high school. Over two thousand students made up the student body, from over a dozen communities in the area. I wasn't surprised that I hadn't known Printz. And I wasn't surprised that Shelley knew who he was. While I was dating Brigham, she'd met people I didn't know. I'd felt a little less guilty about ignoring her, knowing that she was making new friends.

No one said anything for a while. What was there to say? We all wanted to change what had happened, and we couldn't.

Someone had just been mutilated in a mower accident and we had seen the results. That wasn't something we would quickly forget.

We sat on the fountain in the center of the Commons for a long time. And after a while, Donovan surprised me by asking, "Were you working on your lit paper when it happened?"

"No, I wasn't," was all I said.

I could have told them all then, about the disk and how I had the wrong one and how the one I had was full of some stupid code. But it all seemed so unimportant after what had happened to Bob Printz.

"Are you going to work on it now?" Donovan asked me. "I'm through for the day. I was thinking maybe we could take a boat ride on Bottomless Lake. I know you're supposed to be resting, but I'll do all the work, I promise. We should get off campus. You really look like you need to get away, Addie."

Obviously, the sight of all that blood hadn't bothered *him*. My stomach, on the other hand, was in turmoil, churning and chugging like a washing machine. I didn't think riding in a boat would help, especially in a lake that made me very nervous. It was called Bottomless Lake for a very good reason. No one seemed to know for certain just exactly how deep that lake really was, but I'd heard stories about people drowning and their bodies never being recovered. "I have stuff to do," I said. "I still haven't found my purse. As long as I'm out here, I might as well check out lost and found at the administration building. If it's not there, I'll check the stadium again."

"It's not *there*, Addie," Brynne said flatly. "Your purse isn't *at* the stadium. Kirk and I would have found it."

I ignored her. I had a feeling she hadn't looked all that hard. Kirk had probably done most of the searching. "Do any of you know anyone named Redd?" I asked. The name written on the file I'd taken by mistake just suddenly appeared in my head, and then in my mouth, and then jumped out into the air, as if it had a will of its own.

"Just Brynne here," Kirk said, grinning.

"No one calls me Red," she said, scowling. "I don't like nicknames. Besides, 'Red' is a nickname for a trucker or someone who rides a motorcycle or performs in a rodeo. It wouldn't suit *me* at all."

I got up and began walking toward the administration building, a huge white stone building on the other side of campus. The others all followed. When they were beside me, I repeated, "You're all sure you don't know anyone named Redd?"

"Why?" Donovan asked. "Should we?"

"No, I guess not. I just wondered, that's all."

Donovan laughed. "No, you didn't. People don't suddenly get urges to ask other people if they know someone named Redd. You had a reason. What is it?"

So I told them about the disk mix-up after all. I finally realized I couldn't handle this alone. "But," I finished, "my name is on my disk and what I can't figure out is why the owner of the one I took hasn't come to the Quad to trade with me. Wouldn't you think he'd want his material back?"

"I guess you've already looked at his disk," Shelley said, "or you wouldn't have known it wasn't yours. So what's on it?"

I fingered the bandage on my forehead, thinking how much better off I was than Bob Printz. "A bunch of gibberish. Initials, a kind of code, I guess. Didn't make any sense to me, but it looked kind of important. Don't you think it's weird that he hasn't come looking for it?"

We passed the place where Bob Printz's life

had changed forever. All traces of blood were gone, the grass evened out. The spot on the Commons looked exactly as it always had. As if nothing had happened. I looked away.

"Does seem weird that no one's come to you to trade disks," Kirk said. "You could maybe make an announcement over the campus radio station, saying that you have it. They announce lost and found stuff all the time on that station."

"I told you, my name is on the label. He already *knows* my name."

"Maybe he went home for the weekend," Brynne suggested, "and didn't even realize the disk he had wasn't his. If he only figured it out this morning, when he got back, he probably hasn't had time yet to look you up."

For just a second, that seemed possible. I'd taken the disk on Friday, late in the day. If he'd been in a hurry to split, he might have pocketed my disk too quickly to notice the name.

No. That didn't explain the frantic searches in my room and car.

Kirk must have agreed with me. "He'd have checked the disk by now. Last night, probably, getting ready for classes this morning. All he'd have had to do was give Addie a call at the Quad. Why hasn't he done that?"

No one answered him.

They waited on the steps of the administration building while I ran inside to see if my purse had been turned in.

It had. The woman at lost and found handed it to me with a smile.

My driver's license was still there, my keys, and my student ID. But the money was gone. Like I was surprised.

"You were lucky," the woman said. "The person who found your bag took it to your dorm, but you weren't there, so instead of tossing it in a Dumpster, he was nice enough to bring it here."

"Who returned it?" I asked her, realizing that she wasn't aware the money was missing.

"I don't know. I wasn't here. But there was a note on it explaining that he or she had tried to contact you. I thought that was nice."

Obviously, he wasn't the one who had brought the purse to Butler Hall. He'd dumped it, and someone else, someone much nicer, had found it.

Clutching the bag in both hands, I thanked her and left the building. But instead of feeling relieved, I was more uneasy than ever. Getting the bag back just pointed out how easy it was to return things on campus. My name was in my purse. It had been returned. My name was on my disk. But it *hadn't* been returned.

The answer didn't pop into my head all of a sudden. It came in bits and pieces. He . . . hadn't . . . brought the disk back . . . even though he could have, even though my name was on it . . . because . . . because . . .

Because he didn't want to reveal his identity.

It was the only explanation that made any sense. He didn't want me to know who he was.

And the new, frightening question then became . . . *why not?*

Chapter 12

Wrestling with the new, scarier question, but keeping it to myself for now, I led everyone back to the Quad, grateful that I had my purse back, but dreading the call to my sister.

The only cash I had was a few dollars, so I got the call out of the way first. I got lucky. My sister wasn't home. Stokes answered, was very understanding, and promised to wire me cash instead of sending me a check, which would take longer.

The phone call should have eased my queasy stomach. But it didn't. Because the new and alarming question was still there, lurking in my mind like a masked burglar, about to steal what little peace of mind I still had left.

I had something in my possession that someone on campus didn't want me to have. Someone on campus, who, armed with a knife, had flown into a rage in my car and ripped the upholstery to shreds. He didn't want me to have that disk. He had vandalized our room and my car, looking for his property, and of course he was the one who had stolen my purse.

He must have been furious when he came up empty-handed.

And maybe he had also thrown that discus onto the track, in an attempt to draw my friends away from my purse so he could take it and search it for the disk.

And it wasn't over yet. Because I still had the disk.

Hoping my friends would talk me out of the new and frightening thoughts I was having, I shared all of it with them.

Kirk suggested that I call the police, tell them what I suspected.

"And say what?" I asked him. "That I have a disk with a bunch of initials on it?"

"Why don't you just take the disk back to the library and put it where you found it?" Brynne asked. "If it's making you that nervous, get rid of it."

Cam nodded agreement. "Good idea."

But Donovan said, "I think you're reaching here, Addie. There would have to be some pretty heavy-duty stuff on that disk to make someone react the way you're talking about. So what are you thinking the code means?"

"Has to be something pretty uncool. Maybe even criminal. A cheating scheme? A really big-deal cheating scheme?"

"I think Addie has a point," Kirk said.

I was about to send him a grateful glance when I realized with dismay that I didn't *want* anyone agreeing with me. I wanted all of them to react the way Donovan had. I wanted them to tell me I was nuts, overimaginative, over-reacting. And I wanted them to make *me* believe that.

"So far," Kirk continued, "it looks like all he's been trying to do is get the disk back without letting you know who he is. But he hasn't succeeded, has he? You still have the disk. If you're right about any of this, he's going to start getting very nervous, afraid that you've had enough time to figure out his code and discover what he's up to. Couldn't be anything good, or it wouldn't be in code. The longer you hang on to that disk, the more dangerous it is for you."

Shelley let out a little half-laugh. "Addie? Figure out a code? I don't *think* so."

My cheeks burned. I had never made fun of her when she was overweight. Never.

She didn't stop there. "I guess this means the owner of the disk doesn't know our Addie. He must be a total stranger, or he wouldn't be the least bit worried about her deciphering his tricky, secret little code."

I was angry enough to strangle her. "Shelley! You make me sound mentally deficient! I'm *not* stupid!"

She saw my hurt and anger then, and was instantly contrite. "Sorry, Addie. I didn't mean to make it sound like that. You're not stupid. But a code? You had more trouble with logarithms in high school than anyone in class."

If Shelley hadn't said all of that, I probably would have taken Brynne's suggestion and gotten rid of the disk.

I would have, *if* Shelley hadn't made it sound as if I were too stupid to live, in front of friends who didn't know me well enough yet to be sure she was exaggerating. I was so angry, I made up my mind that very second that I was going to figure out the code or die trying.

And when I had the answers, Shelley Karlsen would be the first person I'd tell.

"I think," Cam said as I stomped along the walkway, my head up, my cheeks still hot with anger and humiliation, "that we should all take a look at that disk. What about it, Addie? Maybe one of us can help figure out what it means and why the owner is shy about claiming it in person."

"I don't need any help!" I snapped. "In spite

of what my supposed best friend says."

Shelley coughed nervously. "I said I was sorry, Addie."

"Well, the truth is," Cam added tactfully, "you'd be doing me a favor. I'd like to get a look at it. Codes fascinate me. You wouldn't mind if I just took a quick peek, would you?"

He was being so nice about it. And at least he hadn't implied that I was feebleminded.

"Okay," I said, a little reluctantly. Maybe Cam, with his knowledge of computers, could get me started in the right direction. "Just for a minute, though. I have things to do."

"You're not going out on the lake?" Donovan asked, disappointment in his voice.

"I said I have things to do!"

It would be nice to get some positive attention for a change. And that's what I'd get if I cracked that stupid code and found out that it really was something ominous. I'd be a hero, famous all over campus.

Then I remembered the frenzied attack on Esmerelda's upholstery and wondered if I had truly lost my mind. Because of some stupid little remarks Shelley had made, I was going to attempt to thwart a crazy person?

Maybe he wasn't the crazy one. Maybe I was.

When we got to our room, I went straight

to the pizza box under my bed. Slid the disk free. Sat down in my chair, turned on my computer, and inserted the disk. With everyone standing around me, leaning over my shoulders, I waited for the code to reappear.

It didn't.

Instead, my own words jumped off the screen at me. "Analysis of Charles Dickens's *A Tale of Two Cities*." Beneath that, the words, "By Adelaide Adair."

"Code?" Brynne said from behind me. "That's not code. I can read it just fine. It's plain old English."

I paged through to the end. Through all eight pages, there was nothing but my lit paper.

Until I reached the last page I'd completed. I had written only two paragraphs. The rest of the page had been blank.

Now, written on the screen in capital letters were the words, KURIOSITY KILLED THE KAT.

Feeling a little faint, I leaned back in my wooden chair. When the bizarre message had been permanently imprinted on my brain, I pulled the disk free, and looked at the white label. There they were, my name and the name of my file, just as I'd written them.

"Addie?" Cam said. "That's not the disk you

took by mistake, is it? That's your own disk, am I right?"

I turned around, looked up at the faces around me. "Yes," I answered clearly. "This is my disk, the one I left at the library by mistake. Except for the message at the end. . . . When I ran from this room earlier today, this disk was not here. Which means," looking straight at Shelley, "while we were gone, someone came into our room again. They wouldn't have had to break in, either," I added, remembering. "I rushed out of here after that mower hit Bob without bothering to lock anything. I probably didn't even take the time to shut the door."

Shelley's dark eyes moved automatically to the door, as if she expected to find the culprit still lurking there.

"And the other disk?" Donovan asked. "The one you took by mistake?"

"Gone," I said, knowing I was right without even having to search the room. "It's gone."

Chapter 13

"Well, good!" Brynne exclaimed. "If it's gone, you can relax, Addie. Good riddance, right? Now you don't have to worry about it anymore."

This was true. I had my own disk back, and I didn't have to worry about the coded disk any longer.

So why was I disappointed instead of being relieved?

Because I'd wanted to crack that code. Stupid, I know, especially since, if my theory was right, the guy who had invented that particular code had a loose way with a sharp knife.

What was wrong with me? I should have been happier. It was over now, and the only damage done was two scraped elbows, two bruised and bloodied knees, and a thick, white bandage on my forehead. Compared to what Bob Printz had gone through today and the fate that Potsy had suffered, I'd gotten off easy.

"You're right," I told Brynne. "You're absolutely right." I shut off the computer and stood up. "It's getting late, and the sun won't be out much longer but Donovan, if you still want to go out to the lake, I'm game." Why not? Wasn't I supposed to feel like celebrating, now that the disk mix-up had been straightened out? Any threat that disk had posed was behind me now. Time to party.

I wasn't sorry when no one else wanted to go with us. Brynne said it was too late. Kirk said he had an essay to write. Shelley had a late afternoon class and Cam was playing volleyball at six.

"If everyone else hadn't had other plans," Donovan said as we left campus in his white Trooper, "I would have told them horror stories about Bottomless Lake until they'd chickened out. The whole idea was for the two of us to do something alone for a change."

At the lake, Donovan rented a small white motorboat. When we had settled into it and left the dock, I said, "Did you ever find out what Potsy's real name was?"

He didn't hear me over the motorboat's roar, and I had to lean in closer and shout.

"Yeah!" he shouted back, expertly steering the boat out into the middle of the lake. The sun was descending rapidly, and I was glad I'd brought my heavy blue sweater. The minute the last of the rays were below the horizon, the air would turn cold very quickly. "Donald Jacobs."

"Donald Jacobs?" The name sounded familiar. But I didn't know anyone named Donald, did I? I couldn't remember ever calling anyone "Donald" or "Don" or "Donny." And I'd never known anyone named Potsy. That I *would* remember. "There was a little family store in Shelley's neighborhood, on the corner," I said, thinking aloud. "I think it was called Jacobs. I'll have to ask her. She knew a lot more people in high school than I did."

Donovan wasn't listening. He seemed intent on taking the little boat out as far into the middle as possible, and I began to feel a little nervous about the depth. What if we tipped over? Swimming is one of the few things I actually do well, but rumor had it that this water never, ever warmed up. Anyway, if the temperature didn't get me, the depth would probably panic me. I'm not wild about deep water. Pools are better. You always know where the bottom is.

Unlike Bottomless Lake.

There were few boats out now. I saw only two, on the far side of the lake, moving slowly toward shore, and then another, much larger boat just leaving the dock on our side. Someone going out for a twilight dinner on the water? How romantic.

It was almost completely dark when we reached the middle of the lake. Donovan cut the engine and the boat began bobbing quietly on the water, as if a giant hand hidden beneath the dark surface of the water held it gently, rocking it like a baby's cradle. The only sounds we heard were the occasional toot of a boat's horn as it left or arrived at a dock, and the rhythmic lapping of the water caused by the boat's movement.

"This is really nice," I commented as Donovan brought out a thermos of coffee and a bag of glazed doughnuts. "It's so quiet and peaceful out here." Unlike campus, where people invaded your room and your things, and then slashed your car to pieces in a fit of rage.

We sat in the middle of the boat sipping sweet, hot coffee, eating doughnuts, and talking, for a long time. The sky got darker, the air grew chilly. My sweater was no longer warm enough. But I was so comfortable, sitting beside Donovan, looking out over the water, and I was having such a nice time that I didn't want to see the evening end, so I refused to let myself shiver with cold.

One thing about Donovan, he never once

talked to me as if he suspected I wasn't understanding what he was saying. He talked about becoming an electrical engineer, and discussed what that meant to him without once saying, "Get it?" the way Shelley sometimes did, and the way Brigham almost always had. Of course I "got it." A C, even a D, in math doesn't mean your brain cells have disintegrated, or that you never had any to begin with. It just means you're not too hot at math. Big deal. I'd never had plans to become an accountant, so what did it matter?

And if I had had plans to become an accountant, I would have changed them the very second that Dennis-the-accountant left town with Shelley's mom.

Donovan moved closer, and I forgot about everything that had happened. I forgot about the disk, the bus accident, and the mower running over Bob Printz.

I was so far from reality that when the noise ahead of us broke the silence, I thought it was my imagination. But when it came again, sounding closer this time, I withdrew from Donovan's arms and sat up straight. "Did you hear that?" I asked him. "It sounds like a boat coming this way, but I don't see any lights out there."

He listened. And nodded. "I hear it." He

peered into the black emptiness ahead of us. "Maybe it's just someone over at the dock, warming up or checking their engine." He put his arm around my shoulder again, saying, "Now where were we?"

But I moved forward and squinted my eyes to see if there was anything out on the lake. There was something about that sound . . .

I tried to tell myself that the events of the past few days had set my teeth on edge, set my nerve endings on fire, made me more alert to possible danger because I'd grown to expect it, and I hadn't settled down yet even though the disk was now safely out of my room.

"Donovan? I know there aren't any lights, except for the ones along the docks and that one way over there," I said, pointing, "that's hardly moving. But doesn't it sound to you like something is headed our way? Doesn't it sound like *a boat* is headed straight for us?"

I could see in the reflected glow of our boat's light that he was annoyed, at first. But the noise was growing so much louder, so quickly, that there was no way he could ignore my questions.

He sat up very straight on the seat, staring intently into the darkness. Then he picked up a lantern sitting on the bottom of the boat, lit it with a book of matches he took from his pocket, stood up, leaned out over the side of the boat, holding the lantern high, and looked again.

The sound of a boat's motor . . . the motor of a boat much larger than ours . . . was deafening now, and still there were no lights approaching.

To take a boat out on Bottomless Lake at night without lights is . . . insane. That lake is difficult enough to navigate in the full light of day, or at night with proper lighting. It was because the idea was so insane that it took Donovan and me so long to realize what was happening.

He had been standing up in the boat for only a few seconds when I heard him declare under his breath, "Oh, my God!"

He whipped around, dropping the lantern, and shouted at me. "Get up, get *up!*" Then he threw himself at the ignition. Turned the key. Realized there wasn't time, whirled around, calling my name in a strangled voice. Then, without even looking out over the water again, he shouted, "Jump, Addie, *jump!* Do it *now!* Push off hard with your feet from the side of the boat!"

Jump? Into that dark, freezing water?

Donovan threw himself at me, grabbed me,

and flung both of us, as one person, over the side of the boat.

It was just before we flew out into the air that I saw, over Donovan's shoulder, the boat come out of the darkness like a giant locomotive, its engine churning, creating a wash that would, I knew, make swimming impossible.

The huge white boat with no lights was speeding straight toward us.

That was what I saw just before Donovan propelled both of us out into the cold, black void.

Chapter 14

Pushing with our feet as we left the boat gave us momentum and propelled us farther out into the water.

Donovan was still clutching my right hand as we landed. Weighted down by our clothing and shoes, we sank like stones. I was too terrified to feel the chill as the icy water penetrated my clothing.

Down, down, into that cold, black water. . . .

Then Donovan kicked my leg. I couldn't see him. The water was too black. But I felt the blow to my shin. When I didn't respond, he kicked it again, harder this time, and I roused myself from my shock enough to get the message. It was a signal to me to begin kicking, swimming upward. Before we'd sunk too far. Before it was too late . . .

I tried to obey. But even as my aching lungs were compelling me to burst back onto the surface for air, my sodden clothes and shoes tugged at me, commanding me to sink deeper and deeper.

I had never been in any place as dark and cold as this bottomless pit. And I was terrified.

So I kicked.

We were struggling valiantly upward, Donovan and I, when the wash of the larger boat racing toward us violently churned the water around us into a frothing whirlpool. We were tossed and thrown this way and that. My right hand, still desperately clutching Donovan's, felt as if it were being ripped right off my wrist.

But, I didn't want to let go of Donovan down there in that icy black pit.

The water churned more violently, slamming me back and forth, up and down, sideways. My wrist, my arm, my shoulder were on fire.

I had to let go.

The minute my hand left Donovan's, I was overwhelmed by panic. I almost gave up then and let the water pull me down. I could never struggle out of this icy, violently churning water by myself.

I've never believed that stuff about your life flashing before your eyes when you're about to die. But I can say for a fact that what did happen was, my mind raced, faster than it ever had. In what had to be only a tiny second or two, with the water knocking me around like a prizefighter in a ring, I thought about all the things I still wanted to do, all the people I wanted to see again, including Mary and Stokes, and all of the places in the world that I hadn't seen yet. I wanted to visit the Taj Mahal, I wanted to climb the Eiffel Tower, I wanted to ride in a canal boat in Venice, I wanted, some day, to teach teenagers how to write short stories and essays.

If I let myself sink, none of those things would ever happen.

It was the anger that saved me. The fury. When my racing mind had sped through all of the things I still wanted to do, still wanted to see, I became furious that someone was trying to take all of that away from me.

I began kicking in earnest, aiming my body upward, up, up, up, until at last, just as my lungs seemed about to burst, my head broke the surface. The churning water surrounding me continued to batter me relentlessly as I gulped fresh air into my lungs.

I came up out of the water facing away from our boat. I spun around, calling Donovan's name, but the roar of the bigger boat's engine drowned out the sound.

It was still racing forward, toward our little boat, now bobbing helplessly on the massive waves created by the wash.

The waves had carried me far enough out of the big boat's path during my struggle that I thought I might be safe. But I saw no sign of Donovan. I was treading water, my body freezing, my teeth chattering wildly, trying to call out his name, even though I knew he'd never hear me over the roar of that engine.

Just before the attacking boat hit, I saw Donovan's head pop up out of the water not far from me. He spotted me, took a few deep, hungry breaths, and began swimming toward me.

He had just reached my side, breathing hard, when the boats collided.

There wasn't even that much of a sound as our boat was crushed into kindling. I'd expected the sound of a major collision, as if two cars were smashing together, but it wasn't like that. There was just one sudden, loud, cracking sound, like a bat smacking a home run out of the park, and then all we heard was the big boat's engine as it swept arrogantly past the wreckage.

It hadn't gone far when I saw its lights come on. Mission accomplished, I thought bitterly. You come out of nowhere, like a giant monster rising out of the lake, devour our boat, and now that it's all over and you've succeeded, you dare to turn your lights on. Coward!

As if thumbing its nose at us in a gesture of smug triumph, the big white boat increased its speed then and raced away into the darkness.

We were lucky. The shower of wood fragments that rained down upon us caused no damage. One jagged chunk from our ruined boat landed in the water not far from me, another sideswiped Donovan, hitting the side of his head with very little force and then dropping away to float aimlessly among the waves. The other pieces left us untouched. But the wreckage lay all around us.

"Donovan," I gasped, "I don't think I can make it to shore. It's too far. I'm too cold."

"You can't give up now, Addie," he said. "Not after making it this far. If you were supposed to drown, you never would have come back up."

My brain thought that made sense. But my body, frozen to the bone, was paying no attention, and when I tried to swim, my arms would do nothing but flap uselessly on top of the water.

I'd have given up then, if Donovan hadn't said, "Hold on, someone's coming."

I couldn't even lift my head to look. It was

too heavy. My hair weighs a lot even when it's dry, and now that every long, frizzy strand of it was plumped with water, my head felt like a huge boulder. The bandage from my forehead had floated away. "Someone's coming? Are you sure?" I whispered.

"Yes, I *am* sure. It's a boat, all right. Must have seen or heard the crash out here. They're heading straight for us, Addie. Hang on!"

Impossible. I was so completely cold, all the way through to my bones, that I felt disoriented.

I didn't have enough energy left to even lift a hand.

I did start to sink then, feet first, my body easily, quietly sliding down beneath the surface of the water as if I'd decided to go below to take a nap.

But I wasn't allowed to stay there. Donovan reached down and grabbed the collar of my sweater and yanked me back up to the top. "Addie, please, just hang on another minute or two!" he shouted. I didn't hear him. I didn't hear anything. I was completely lost to my strange, new world of blackness.

I don't remember being pulled into the rescue boat, don't remember anything until much later when Donovan and I were sitting side by side on the dock, wrapped in warm, dry blankets and sipping steaming hot coffee. It took me a long time to realize that I wasn't still in the lake, that I was safe now, and so was Donovan.

When the police arrived, they directed all of their questions to Donovan, apparently realizing that I was not even able to speak.

"Whose boat was that?" Donovan was asking when I finally snapped out of my frozen trance. "The one that hit us, whose was it?"

"Belongs to Jess Dobbs," the old man who owned the boat rental answered. "But that wasn't Jess drivin' it. Someone stole it. I was down at that last dock there, helpin' someone bring their boat in for the night, and when I come back, I heard Dobbs's boat takin' off across the water. Knew it was that boat, right off, 'cause of the way the engine sounds. Jess souped it up some. He likes speed. Jess, he's gonna have a fit, I can tell you. Takes real good care of that boat. Prob'ly blame me for not keepin' an eye on it, but we never have had a boat stole here, and that's the truth."

"It didn't have any lights on," Donovan said. "That damn boat seemed to come out of nowhere, headed straight for us, as if he knew we were out there and intended from the beginning to hit us. We almost didn't see it in time."

I did speak then. Slowly, as if I were recovering from a long illness. "Donovan's right. It *was* aiming straight at us. On purpose. He *meant* to run us down. Why else would he have had all of his lights off?"

Donovan glanced over at me. "Well, it's not like he knew who we were, Addie. Some jerk out to clobber a smaller boat, that's all. I mean, how could he know who was in our boat?"

"Oh, he could know if he wanted to," the boat rental man said. He pointed to a clipboard hanging from a string on the outside wall of his little white shed. "It's all right there on that sheet of paper. Who took out what boat. People come sometimes, want to know who's out on the water, see if their friends are, and I can't be answering questions all day, so I keep the chart right there." He nodded his graying head. "Yep, he coulda known you was in that boat. Prob'ly did. Prob'ly knew the whole time he was aimin' for you that it was you two."

He got up, walked over to the shed, removed the clipboard, and brought it back to where we were sitting. "You Donovan McGarry?" he asked.

Donovan nodded.

Then the boat rental man hefted the clipboard, looked straight at me with his thick, gray eyebrows furrowed and said, "Then you must be Addie Adair." He tapped the paper with the tip of the pencil in his hand. "Says so right here."

I half turned to look at Donovan. "You put my name on there, too?"

"It's the rules," the rental man said. "Got to have the names of everyone in any boat that's rented. Just in case, you understand. Never know, right? You take tonight, for instance. You two go out in a boat, water's nice and quiet, but somethin' nasty happens. You was lucky, you two. You hadn't a been so lucky, I'd have to know who you was, right? Notify the family, and all that."

My name was on that sheet? *My* name?

All of the lake water that I'd swallowed, along with three glazed doughnuts and two cups of coffee, began to boil up out of my stomach and into my throat and before I could stop it, it erupted out onto the deck, narrowly missing the shoes of the policeman standing closest to me.

I knew it wasn't the lake water that was making me sick, or the doughnuts and coffee. What was making me sick was the knowledge that the person driving that big white boat had known that I, Addie Adair, was sitting in the little white boat. Addie Adair was sitting in the little white boat that he fully intended to splinter into tiny little pieces.

He had seen that sheet of paper, I was convinced. And had come out onto the water looking for us. For me.

He had wreaked havoc in my room, vandalized my car, stolen my purse, tossed a discus in my path on the track, and now he had smashed a boat I'd been sitting in only minutes before he blasted it to kingdom come.

Curiosity had come very close to killing the cat.

Chapter 15

"I don't get it," I said to Donovan as the boat rental agent drove us back to campus. We were still wrapped in the gray blankets. They helped, but our clothing underneath was sodden and clammy, clinging to our skin. I couldn't stop shaking, but I knew that was from fear as much as it was from being cold. "What's going on? I thought all of the horrible things that had happened to me was because I had the disk and someone wanted it back. But he *has* it back now. I don't have it anymore. Why would he try to kill me *now*?"

"I don't know," Donovan said wearily, "I'm too bummed to think about it now." He had been too exhausted to drive the trooper back to campus. "Can't we figure this out tomorrow?"

Donovan had his arm around my shoulders, which would have felt nice except that his windbreaker was soaking wet, which made his arm seem as heavy as a bowling ball.

"I need an answer *tonight*," I said. "Why was our boat smashed to smithereens when I don't even have the disk anymore?"

"You don't know that it had anything to do with the disk."

"Donovan! I may not be the most popular person on campus. I realize that I'm not a cheerleader or president of the student body. But I do not go around campus making enemies. There is *no* chance that what happened tonight isn't connected to that disk. I just can't figure out why, now that I don't have the stupid thing anymore." I slumped down in the seat, so tired my body ached. "I would have given it back if he'd asked for it. It's not my fault he's hiding something and doesn't want me to know who he is."

"Or she."

"What?"

"You have absolutely no reason to believe this character is a guy. It just makes you feel better to think that."

I told myself that Donovan had just taken a long, icy bath in a very deep lake, and that if it hadn't been for him kicking me as I was sinking, I might be at the bottom of that lake right now. And forever. "I don't want to have this argument. It's stupid." Then I leaned against his chest to show him that I wasn't mad, and closed my eyes.

Trying to tell Shelley what had happened when we arrived back at the Quad wasn't easy. She kept saying, "The lake? You fell into the lake?" as if she couldn't comprehend what I was telling her.

I explained again. This time, she said, "What happened to your bandage? Yuck, your forehead looks gross!"

She just wasn't getting it. And I was too tired to keep going over it.

Donovan left, saying he'd call me later. I knew he was, like me, anxious for a hot shower and dry clothes. I took the time to give him a quick kiss on the cheek and say, "Thanks for not letting me give up out there." Watching him walk down the hall toward the stairs, the gray blanket still wrapped around his shoulders, I thought how lucky I was that he hadn't drowned in Bottomless Lake.

When I came out of the bathroom twenty minutes later, a white towel wrapped turban-style around my hair, Shelley tossed a plaid flannel shirt and a pair of jeans at me. "The warmest thing I could find," she said. "They're mine, but you can wear them."

"Thanks, but I'm not going to get dressed

now, Shelley." I sat down on my bed, yanking the covers over my legs and lap, and began rubbing my hair with the towel. "It's late. I'm not going anywhere except to bed. Maybe if I pile on enough blankets, I can actually get warm."

She moved to put the shirt back in the closet, and that was when I noticed the plaid. Orange and yellow and brown and rust. I'd never seen Shelley wearing the shirt. The plaid wasn't a common one. I wouldn't have forgotten seeing it on her before. The long-sleeved, flannel shirt looked much too big for her. A leftover from her heavier days? Was that where I'd seen it? Because *I had* seen it. Somewhere.

She moved to the closet to return the clothes, talking breathlessly about how she couldn't believe we had actually been run down by another boat and asking me if the police had any clues as to who had done it. "Doesn't seem like there's any safe way to travel around campus these days," she commented as she sat down on her bed and picked up the book she'd been reading. "Can't take a boat because someone might run you down, and walking isn't safe because you could be attacked by a runaway lawn mower, and you can't take the shuttle because it could slam right into you and flatten you . . ."

It was when she said that last part that I remembered where I'd seen that plaid shirt. Or at least part of it. I'd seen it on one of the three arms waving in the air just before Potsy toppled over in front of the bus. The other two arms, bare except for the short sleeves of a white T-shirt, had been Potsy's, I was sure of that. The other arm, the third arm, had been reaching out toward Potsy in what I'd thought had been an effort to save him.

"Where did you get that shirt?" I asked Shelley.

"What shirt?"

"That plaid one you just offered me. Is it yours?"

"No. It seemed like the warmest thing in the closet, and you looked so cold, I thought it might help."

"Whose is it?"

"Cam loaned it to me. That silk blouse I bought wasn't nearly warm enough, so he took off his shirt and put it around me. All he had on was a T-shirt, and I know he had to be cold, but he said he wasn't. Isn't that sweet?"

Shelley had never called a boy "sweet" in all the years I'd known her. It sounded weird coming from her mouth. "That shirt is his?"

"And I'm going to keep it forever. He doesn't need it. He has tons of shirts. His closet probably has more clothes in it than mine. He's not exactly poor, Addie."

It made sense that the shirt was Cam's. He'd been right there, at the curb, when Potsy was flattened by that bus. Shelley had said he'd tossed his windbreaker over the victim the minute he saw what had happened. So he had to have been right there. Had he been wearing the plaid shirt? I couldn't remember.

I remembered something else then. Potsy's last name. Donovan had said it was Jacobs. "Shelley, wasn't there a store in your neighborhood owned by some people named Jacobs? Was Potsy related to them?"

"Yes, there was a store. Martin and Esther Jacobs owned it. They used to give everyone red licorice when we went in there. They retired and moved to Florida. There's a gas station there now.

"But," Shelley continued, "I never heard them mention anyone named Potsy. What was his real name?"

"Donald."

Her eyes widened. "You're kidding! The Potsy who got hit by the shuttle bus was Donald Jacobs?"

I nodded. "Why? Do you know him? I mean, did you?"

"Yeah, sure. Or did. A long time ago. He's

their grandson. The Jacobs'. Used to come visit them all the time when he was little. But no one called him Potsy. We all called him Donald. That's what his grandparents called him. Must have picked up the nickname in high school. He quit coming around when he was nine or ten. Must have decided his grandparents were boring."

I thought about that for a minute. "He didn't go to Wickley, too, did he?"

"Sure, he must have. I never ran into him, but there's only one private high school in Braddock, and Donald's parents didn't have the money to send him to private school."

"I don't remember anyone named Donald from high school. But he did look a little familiar when I first saw him in math class."

"I guess he wasn't very memorable. I hadn't seen him in so long, I wouldn't have known him if he'd walked right up to me."

I didn't answer right away. My brain was so waterlogged, I couldn't think straight. But it didn't take an I.Q. in the stratosphere to realize the coincidence here. "Well, don't you think it's really weird that three people from our area were all killed or injured in accidents recently?"

Shelley hadn't made the connection. I could tell by the confusion in her eyes. "What are you talking about?"

"Well, Potsy — Donald — was from back there, and he was killed at the bus stop."

"That was an accident."

"So everyone said." I settled back against the wall. "Then Bob Printz, the one you said went to Wickley with us, was almost chopped to pieces by a maniacal lawn mower. That's two."

"Also an accident. But who's the third one?"

Duh. And she'd made fun of my powers of deduction? "Shelley! You're *looking* at the third one! Someone threw a discus in front of me when I was running the relay, and tonight someone rammed a boat that I had been sitting in only seconds earlier and turned it into matchsticks. If Donovan hadn't seen the boat coming when he did, we'd both be fish food."

"Maybe the guy in the boat just didn't see you out there on the water."

"Shelley, we had a *light* on. *He* didn't. Who goes out on the water at night without lights on? Besides, he stole the boat. The boat rental guy said so."

"Addie, you didn't even *know* Donald Jacobs or Robert Printz, you said so yourself. So how could any of this stuff be connected? And tonight could have been an accident, too. You don't know anything about boats, and neither do I. You said you talked to the police. Let them figure it out."

I stared at her. She hadn't even seemed to be listening to what I'd said about the three of us all being from the same area. That had to mean something. But what? I didn't even know Robert Printz and Donald "Potsy" Jacobs.

I also didn't know what Bob Printz's middle name was, but I wondered if Donald Jacobs had been named for his grandfather. Could Martin be his middle name? That would definitely make him DMJ. The first set of initials on the disk.

I was too nervous and scared to sleep, so I grabbed a piece of paper and a pencil from the table beside my bed, and scribbled out the message I'd found on the disk I'd accidentally taken from the library.

I may not be a mathematical wizard, but I have a terrific memory, especially for anything that intrigues me. I had seen only one picture of the Taj Mahal in my life, but I could have painted a picture of it that would have been reasonably accurate, because I was so impressed by it that it stayed in my mind like a photograph, every detail complete.

Just like I remembered the code on the disk.
DMJ: CRD. SHBAX. NIXQSSKD.
RLP: MWRAX. MNT MN BLD.
CAY: DD. NIXQSSKD.

MC: NHSS. FKSCD. NT. FIN.

I printed the whole message in capital letters, just as I'd seen it on the computer screen. With the paper lying on my lap, I plugged in my hair dryer and while it whirred around me, I studied the letters until my eyes felt like they were bleeding.

It was still gibberish.

But I knew something now that I hadn't known when I first saw it. I knew Potsy's real name. Donald Martin (maybe) Jacobs. DMJ.

And what about RLP? Robert Printz? Robert . . . Leo? . . . Lester? . . . Lucas? Printz?

I could ask Shelley, but she probably wouldn't know Bob's middle name. If she had known him well enough to know his middle name, I would have known him, too.

I shut off the hair dryer and sat up very straight. Two sets of initials belonged to a boy who was dead now and another who'd been maimed.

Everyone thought that both incidents had been accidental.

What were the odds that two people whose names were part of a weird computer message would be victims of accidents only hours apart?

About a million to one, maybe.

My hands holding the piece of paper began to shake. What had I come across here?

I added to those overwhelming odds the fact that the author of that message seemed determined to keep anyone from learning his identity. So determined that, unless I was wrong about that big white boat, he was even willing to *kill* the one person who might have seen his disk message. Me.

DMJ . . . Potsy, who had been run over by a shuttle bus and killed.

RLP . . . Bob Printz, who had been mutilated by a runaway lawn mower.

Could Donald Jacobs have been *pushed* in front of that bus at exactly the right moment?

And had the maintenance man been telling the truth when he'd protested his innocence? Could someone *else* have deliberately shifted the gears on that mower and somehow aimed it straight for Bob Printz?

It seemed to me that I was looking at a list. Not notes for an essay or a paper or an assignment of any kind, but a list.

A list of names.

Remembering Potsy's still, waxen-faced body lying beside the wheels of the shuttle bus, and Bob's blood-chilling scream as the mower sliced away at his feet, my teeth began chattering.

Because I knew then, as surely as I knew my own name, that what I was looking at was a list of *victims*.

Chapter 16

My eyes flew back to the piece of paper in my hands. I scanned it quickly for any sign of my own initials. When I didn't see them at first glance, I looked again, and then again, just to be sure.

"AA" wasn't there.

But I'd already *been* a victim. So why wasn't I on the list?

It wasn't that hard to figure out. The list had been written *before* I ever saw the disk. The names on it had nothing to do with me.

But I was being targeted now. Because the disk's author knew I'd had his nasty little list in my possession. And he didn't dare gamble that I hadn't seen it, hadn't looked at the disk, hadn't figured out his code.

I was a threat to him.

Had Potsy and Bob also been a threat to him? Look what had happened to them.

I was having trouble catching my breath. And the paper in my hands was flapping noisily because my hands were shaking.

The whole thing wasn't my fault. It was *his*. If he'd come to me the minute he realized what had happened at the library, before I'd ever had a chance to see that disk, and traded mine for his, I never would have known anything. Not even when the accidents began happening.

Even with the list, I might not have connected the initials to the accidents, if the disk's owner hadn't behaved the way he had. But instead of coming to me right away, he'd hidden his identity, invaded our room to search it, trashed my car, sabotaged my run on the track, stolen my purse and, tonight, had deliberately tried to kill me.

I knew, now, why he'd aimed that boat at us last night. Because he was afraid that I'd cracked his stupid code and figured out what he was up to. He had to get rid of me, or whatever it was he was planning would be ruined.

Now I *had* to figure out the rest of the code. Before someone else got hurt. Before *I* did.

There were more names on that list: CAY, MC. What did he have in store for them?

I had to stop it.

I didn't know what to do. Who could I go to with my theory who wouldn't laugh at me?

Someone who would at least listen. Not the police. I didn't have enough to go on. Shelley? Fat chance. Too much of a skeptic. Donovan? Maybe.

I lay back against the pillow, my body exhausted and aching from my battle against the cold waters of Bottomless Lake. I held the paper up in front of my eyes and read the other sets of initials again.

CAY. MC. Did I know anyone with those initials?

Names of people on campus danced around me like gremlins, teasing and taunting me. I was too tired to think. I was safe here, in my room at the Quad, with the door locked and my roommate close at hand. I had to sleep now. I'd think about all of it tomorrow, about what it meant and about what I should do with what I knew so far.

Exhausted, I slipped over the edge and disappeared into a darkness that was far more peaceful and safe than the darkness of the lake water had been.

When I woke up the next morning, feeling bruised and battered, Shelley was already gone, her bed a jumble of blankets and sheets. She had left me a note on the dresser, saying she was going to a study session at Nightmare Hall after classes and wouldn't be back until late. "Why don't you come, too?" she'd added at the bottom.

I called one of the policemen who had questioned Donovan and me on the dock to see if they'd learned anything about the stolen boat.

Yes, he said, they had found it. Abandoned in a cove several miles away from where we'd been attacked. But they hadn't found the thief who had stolen it and rammed our boat. He had no more information than that.

I hesitated, thinking how little I had to go on, but couldn't help saying finally, "About the shuttle bus accident and the mower accident on campus? You . . . you don't have any reason to believe they weren't just plain old accidents, do you?"

He said no, they had no reason to think they were anything but accidental, although the runaway mower was a puzzler. The maintenance man, he said, was still insisting the machine was defective. Then the officer added, "Any particular reason why you asked me that question? You know something about those incidents?"

That scared me. I didn't want him coming to the Quad to ask me a lot of questions. The disk's owner might be watching me, might see a policeman arrive to talk to Addie Adair. That would not be good. "No," I said, "I don't know anything. I just wondered, that's all. Two accidents on campus so close together, it just seemed weird."

"Exactly what we thought. And we're still checking out the mower thing. And following up on your boat accident last night. If you hear anything that you think would help, you let us know, okay?"

I said of course I would, and hung up. But I was mad. My "boat accident"? Was that what they were calling it? If that was an accident, I was a mathematical genius.

I could have told him about the initials on the disk, but I didn't see what good that would do. I didn't even know who that disk belonged to. And I still didn't have a clue about the rest of the code.

As soon as I'd hung up, I felt abandoned and vulnerable again. Talking to a law enforcement official had made me feel momentarily safe. If someone had come into the room just then and lunged at me, maybe with a knife, I could have screamed into the telephone and help would have been on its way. But now . . .

I didn't want to go to class. The thought of leaving my room, of being out there on campus, exposed and unprotected, while *he* was out there, made my breath catch in my throat. I fought the urge to rush to the window, fling it open, and scream at the top of my lungs, "I don't *have* your stupid disk anymore, and I don't know what your stupid code means, so *leave me alone!*"

Anyway, one more day off wouldn't hurt. I'd make up the work later. I'd stay here, safe and sound. I was going to study that list until I came up with some answers.

If I didn't have any luck, I'd take it to the study session later at Nightmare Hall and see if anyone else had any ideas about what the letters meant.

I had no luck at all. Although I went over and over that list a hundred, maybe a thousand times until my brain was reeling and my eyes felt swollen, I came up with no more answers.

Anger overcame my fear then. Why should I make myself a prisoner? At two o'clock, I dressed in jeans and a short-sleeved white turtleneck shirt, put my hair in a ponytail to keep it out of my eyes, checked the clean, dry bandage on my forehead to make sure it was in place, and left the room, locking the door securely behind me.

I practically raced down the stairs to the lobby, half-expecting someone to jump out at me with a knife raised over my throat.

I left the building with a sigh of relief. There were people walking across campus, so it seemed safer than the deserted staircase. I was intent on finding Shelley or Donovan or Brynne or Kirk, even Cam. I would make sure I was with other people until we left campus for Nightingale Hall. No one would be dumb enough to attack me when I was in a group.

But . . . Potsy had been in a crowd when he'd been pushed off that curb, hadn't he?

I pushed that nasty thought out of my mind and hurried across the Commons.

There was a new chill in the air that matched my mood, and the sky was the color of sidewalks. Autumn was finally hitting the campus of Salem University.

I'd brought a denim jacket, just in case, and slipped it on as I walked. My arms, still sore from last night's ordeal, squealed a protest. It was getting cold, but nothing could be colder than last night's water. Maybe I'd just get pneumonia from my encounter with the lake, and die that way. Then he wouldn't have to kill me.

Kill me? Did I really believe that someone wanted to kill me?

The thought made my skin crawl now that I was out in the open. I felt like one of those wooden brown bears travelling across a shelf in a shooting gallery at a carnival, just waiting to be knocked down by the ping of an air rifle.

Cam, Donovan, Brynne, and Shelley were sitting in the rec center dining hall drinking coffee and talking about last night's attack out on the lake. Cam and Shelley seemed to be convinced that it had been accidental, that the bigger boat simply hadn't seen us.

When I'd ordered and received my own coffee and half a tuna sandwich, I took a seat beside Donovan. "And how," I asked after taking a quick sip to get sugar into my system, "do you explain the fact that the boat was stolen?" I needed to tell them what was going on, but not here, not in the rec center with people all around. It would have to wait.

"Well, that's why we think it was an accident," Shelley said. "The guy was obviously out for a joyride, didn't see you, and then panicked after he hit you."

"Without lights?" I asked harshly. I hadn't eaten anything but a handful of crackers since noon, and I was feeling very light-headed, and very irritable.

"Haven't eaten anything lately, have you?" Shelley asked me, rolling her eyes toward the ceiling. "Honestly, Addie, you never learn!" To Cam, she said, "She has low blood sugar. She's supposed to eat every so often, but she forgets."

"Please don't do that!" I snapped. "Please do not discuss me as if I were not in the room. I *am eating*." I held up my sandwich for all to see.

"Sorry," Shelley muttered, but she didn't sound sorry. "Are you coming to our study session at Nightmare Hall?"

"Yes," I answered, "I am coming to the study session." I'd tell them my theory about the codes on the disk there. That seemed appropriate. Nightmare Hall looked like the kind of place where people could talk about being killed without anyone calling them crazy. But that wasn't the real reason I was going to the study session. I was also going because I had absolutely no intention of going back to the room by myself. He'd been in that room twice. There was nothing to stop him from coming in a third time.

Kirk had a late lab so we didn't leave campus for Nightingale Hall until after five. It was already getting dark, but I felt safe in a car filled with people. This was much better than sitting alone in my room watching from my window as darkness swallowed up the campus and terror did the same to me.

The letters "CAY" and "MC" danced before my eyes as we pulled up the long, gravel driveway to the gloomy old house up on the hill above the highway. Whose initials were they? Who was next?

Had to be me, "AA," even though I wasn't on the list. He had probably added my initials as soon as he had the disk back in his vicious little hands.

As we got out of the car at the top of that tree-shadowed hill, the wind whistling around us, Donovan said, "I need to talk to you later, okay?"

We had the big, high-ceilinged library all to ourselves. The housemother, Mrs. Coates, had gone to a concert in town, and the other residents were still on campus, Donovan informed us.

The room was so cold, Donovan and Kirk worked at starting a fire in the huge stone fireplace and the rest of us sat on the faded Oriental rug surrounded by books and papers or on the worn, overstuffed furniture. Brynne and I chose the floor; Shelley and Cam chose the couch. When the fire had begun warming the room, Donovan took a seat beside me and Kirk sank to the floor next to the fireplace and Brynne.

Everyone except me started studying. I tried. I borrowed Cam's notes from lit class. They were neat and legible. I was impressed.

Good-looking, and smart, too. Lucky Shelley.

But concentrating was impossible. I couldn't get that list out of my head, and I found myself continually glancing around to make sure the only people in the room were people I trusted. I had to make sure that no one intent on taking my life had somehow sneaked in while I wasn't looking.

Brynne quietly quizzed Kirk on his Civil War material, Shelley and Cam lay on the couch facing each other, reading, and Donovan and I worked on notes.

The list was burning a hole in the back pocket of my jeans, but I decided to wait until we took a break. I wanted their full attention. Besides, I hadn't figured out yet exactly how to begin. "Hey, guys, wait'll you see what I came up with," didn't seem like the right way to go. I needed to think of something better.

We'd been studying for about an hour when the silence was broken by the most awful sound. A shrill, high whistle. It seemed to be screaming throughout the house.

Everyone sat upright, eyes wide and questioning.

"Smoke alarm," Donovan yelled, and jumped to his feet. We all did the same.

Barking orders, Donovan dispatched each of us to a different room, some upstairs, some downstairs, to seek out the source of the smoke, if there was any. "Sometimes it just goes off for no reason," he added as he turned to pound up the stairs toward the attic. Kirk and Cam followed, while Shelley, Brynne, and I took the first floor.

I hesitated in the hall while everyone else ran in different directions. I didn't want to go *anywhere* alone in that shadowy old house, but the others were following Donovan's orders and I didn't want to act like a wimp. Shelley had said to check the kitchen, which was on the first floor, so it wasn't as if I had all that far to go. Besides, I was in the house with my friends. There were no strangers here.

I saw no sign of smoke or fire in the kitchen. It was long and narrow and dimly lit. A wall of windows behind the sink on the far wall overlooked the back yard. For just a second, as I stood in the doorway, I thought I saw something moving out there. But it was so dark, I couldn't really see, and besides, everyone was still inside.

Becoming braver, I moved into the kitchen and checked around. No smoke. No fire. And since I hadn't heard anyone shout, "Fire!" I had already decided the horrible sound had been a false alarm. I turned around and made my way back down the dark, tunnel-like hallway to the library.

Since our concentration had already been broken, this seemed like a good time, if everything really was okay in the house, to tell them all what I'd discovered about the disk.

Brynne was waiting in the doorway. "False alarm?" she asked, and I answered, "Looks like."

"So where's Michelle?" she asked me.

"Michelle?"

"Your best friend and roommate. Forgotten her name already? She hasn't been gone *that* long."

"Oh." A common mistake. Lots of people made it. "Shelley's full name isn't Michelle. It's Rochelle."

She didn't believe me, I could tell. "You're kidding."

"No, I'm not. She hates it, though. So she tells everyone her name is Shelley."

"Well, she might at least have told me her name was Rochelle," Brynne said angrily.

I shrugged. "What's the difference? You'd still have to call her Shelley."

Donovan loped down the stairs a few minutes later, his face filled with relief, saying, "I guess it was just a glitch in the smoke alarm. No smoke, no flames. We're okay."

Kirk came down the stairs, followed a few minutes later by Cam. Neither had found any sign of smoke.

But Shelley still hadn't returned. "Where'd you send Shelley, Donovan?" I asked him.

"Mrs. Coates's bedroom. Just off the kitchen."

"Off the kitchen? I was back there. I didn't see her." Because I'd been so hesitant to investigate earlier, Shelley had left the library before I did. But I should have seen her when I was in the kitchen.

We waited there in the doorway, but she didn't come back.

Cold fingers crawled up my spine. Shelley's name wasn't on that list, but . . .

We waited five more minutes. Then, searching singly again because it would go faster, we looked in every room in the house. But there was no sign of her.

"She couldn't have just disappeared!" an annoyed Brynne said when we all met again at the foot of the stairs.

But she *had* disappeared. Shelley Karlsen, who had come into the chilly, shadowed old house with us, was no longer *with* us.

She was gone.

And if I made a little sound then, a little

groan or a gasp, if my face drained of color and I sagged a little against the door frame, it was because we were in Nightmare Hall, a place where people had *died*, and my best friend and roommate was missing.

Chapter 17

I had been so sure that I would be the next victim.

Shelley's name wasn't even on that list.

"Well, where did she *go*?" Brynne asked, glancing around as if she expected to find the answer written on someone's face. "Addie, you know her better than we do. Does she have a thing about fire? Maybe the smoke alarm scared her and she ran out of the house."

"Everyone has a thing about fire, Brynne," I answered. I could feel my legs trembling, I was so frightened for Shelley. "And no, Shelley wouldn't have just run out of the house, not while the rest of us were still in here." I hesitated, and then added, "I think we should call the police."

That stunned them. They'd all been thinking that Shelley had simply left of her own free will. I knew better.

Donovan was the first to say, "The police?"

I told them all then, as quickly as I could, conscious of the passing minutes, what I had discovered about the computer disk, and what I thought it meant.

It must have blown them away, because when I'd finished, no one said anything.

Then Brynne said, her voice thick with disbelief, "You're just guessing. You can't possibly be sure that you're right. It's too bizarre."

"I'm right," I said firmly. "I am. Except for thinking that I would be his next victim, because he'd have to stop me from blowing the whistle on him. I still can't figure out why he would do anything to Shelley. She isn't even on that list."

I was looking at Brynne as I spoke, and even as I finished the last sentence, I remembered Brynne saying, "Michelle." Michelle . . . meaning Shelley, whose real name was Rochelle, a fact that almost no one on campus knew.

The initials "MC" on the list flashed before my eyes. "MC." What if, like Brynne, the disk's owner thought Shelley's name was Michelle? And . . . my mind was racing now . . . and her last name . . . Karlsen. She was Swedish. But the much more common spelling was "Carlson." Wouldn't it be natural to assume, when you heard "Karlsen," that it was spelled with a C?

It would.

Rochelle Karlsen. Michelle Carlson. MC.

"Oh, my God," I whispered, moving away from the door frame. "I was wrong! Shelley *is* on that list!"

They were all staring at me. "What?" Kirk said.

"He just didn't know how to *spell* it!" I cried. "We have to *find* her!"

"You're that sure that what you saw is a list?" Cam asked me, his eyes anxious. "A list of victims?"

"Yes!" I shouted, "yes, I am! I *know* that's what it is, and I know that Shelley's name is on it. I was stupid, I should have realized . . . we have to call the police." I was screaming now. "Help me, help me find her!"

Donovan must have seen something in *my* face then, because without a word, he turned and moved to a telephone in the hall, picked it up and dialed 911.

But before he had even begun speaking into the receiver, I was running down the hall toward the kitchen and the back door. "She's not in the house," I shouted over my shoulder, "so we have to look outside. Hurry!"

And although Brynne complained that it was cold and dark out there, I could hear them following me.

I didn't even stop to look for a flashlight.

The minute I stepped outside, I began shouting Shelley's name. My voice rose higher and higher as I stumbled along in the dark, looking behind the wood box and behind trees and bushes and lawn furniture for any sign of her.

I found the locket halfway to a small, squat structure at the rear of the property, just at the edge of the wooded hill. I would never have seen the piece of jewelry in all that darkness, but I stepped on something that didn't feel like a rock or stone. I bent down and picked it up, looked down at it just as I had on the Commons when I'd found it there.

"It's Shelley's locket," I said as Donovan caught up with us. "She had it on when she left the room this morning."

Donovan said, "Cops are on their way. All I told them was that we couldn't find someone. Didn't waste any time filling them in. We'll do that when they get here."

"I told you she must have run out of the house," Brynne said, looking down at the locket in my extended palm. "Probably panicked when she heard that smoke alarm. Only," she lifted her head, glancing around, "where is she now? She wouldn't have gone all the way back to campus, would she? Without making sure the rest of us were okay?"

"No," I said, "she wouldn't have." My voice was heavy with fear. "She's out here somewhere. I think we should check out the barn or whatever it is." I pointed to the small building ahead of us. It looked fairly new.

"The new shed," Donovan said, moving in that direction. "Old one burned down. Someone died in the fire."

I moved right alongside him, as fast as he, but my stomach rolled over when he mentioned a death.

"She wouldn't be in there," Brynne protested even as she followed. "Why would she be in there? She has to know we're looking for her. She should be standing right out here where we can see her."

She would be if she could, was my immediate reaction, and then I really felt sick. Because I knew I was right. Shelley wouldn't have panicked at the sound of the smoke alarm, she wouldn't have run out of the house.

So the reason she wasn't here was, she *couldn't* be. It was that simple. And that terrifying.

Donovan pulled open the wide door to the barn, which slid on a track.

We stepped inside. It was dark, and still smelled of fresh-cut lumber.

"Shelley?" I said, not really expecting an answer, because if she could have answered, she would have answered when I first began screaming her name out in the yard. "Shelley? Are you in here?"

Someone lit a match and held it up. At first, it didn't help, but as the yellow-red glow spread, it provided just enough light to see a few feet in front of us. But that was enough.

Her feet, clad only in white socks, were dangling directly in front of us.

Her shoes had dropped off and were lying on the bare wood floor beneath her.

My heart stopped, and I looked up, although I didn't, *didn't* want to.

She was there, hanging by a rope around her neck from a wooden rafter. Her arms, orange in the turtleneck sweater she was wearing under the plaid flannel shirt Cam had loaned her, the sleeves rolled to the elbow, hung lifelessly at her sides. Her head drooped at an odd angle, resting on her left shoulder.

But she wasn't looking at us.

Her eyes were closed.

The match went out.

I began screaming.

Chapter 18

I couldn't stop screaming. "Get her down, get her down, someone, please!"

Brynne, murmuring, "Oh no, oh no," searched frantically for a light switch and found one. She flicked it on and the barn was flooded with light.

That made it worse. We could see so much better. I didn't want to see.

"Take her *down*!" I screamed again.

Donovan and Kirk moved, running to get a ladder standing against the wall of the barn. They ran to place the ladder beneath Shelley. As Donovan scrambled up the rungs, he yanked a pocketknife from his jeans and snapped it open.

The barn was small, the rafter not that far above us. One quick slash with the knife and Shelley plummeted. Kirk was standing directly beneath her. She landed with a soft whooshing sound in his arms.

I heard sirens screaming up the driveway.

As Kirk lay Shelley on the wood floor and Donovan came back down the ladder, Brynne ran outside to direct the police to the barn.

"She's not dead," Donovan said harshly as he knelt beside Shelley and felt for a pulse. "Addie, she's still alive."

I hung back, my hands over my mouth to stop the screams. I knew he was lying. How could she not be dead? The way her head had hung, at that crazy angle. Her neck had to be broken. She couldn't be alive.

The police officer who at Brynne's direction had already called for an ambulance on his car radio, assured us, when he had checked her pulse, that Shelley was alive. "Needs to be taken to the hospital in town, though," he said.

I wasn't listening. I was staring at that plaid flannel shirt. Shelley had borrowed it from Cam. It was the same shirt that I'd seen on the arm waving near Potsy just before he tumbled beneath that shuttle bus. I'd thought, when she told me that, that Cam's arm had been reaching out in an attempt to *save* Potsy.

What if it hadn't been? What if, instead, it had been reaching out to *push* him?

"Looks like a suicide note here," one of the officers said, fishing a piece of paper out of Shelley's shirt pocket.

I stood very still. Suicide? Shelley? Never. If she was going to do that, she'd have done it when her mother took a hike with Dennis-the-accountant. She never, never would.

I moved closer, stared down at the type-written note as the officer read aloud, " *'I'm sorry for what I did. Forgive me. Michelle.'* "

I clapped my hands together. I jumped up and down. I laughed, a harsh, cruel sound that echoed throughout the barn. "Idiot!" I shrieked with glee, stomping back and forth on the wood floor, my flats making a sharp, clicking sound. "What an idiot! Can't even sign the right name to a fake suicide note!" I whirled to face the people kneeling beside Shelley. They were all staring at me as if I'd suddenly sprouted antennae. "Her name is *Rochelle, Rochelle!*" I shouted in triumph. "She wouldn't sign the wrong name to her own suicide note. That *proves* that someone *hung* her up there. Shelley would never try to kill herself. I knew it."

The officers promised to investigate thoroughly, and I thought I saw regret in Donovan's eyes. Because he hadn't taken me seriously enough?

Now he would.

My brain whirled as the policemen gave Shelley CPR, as she began to respond, stirring and moving restlessly and then coughing. I couldn't stop thinking about the plaid shirt.

There were people on campus who had been surprised when Cameron Truro, handsome, popular, rich, athletic, had begun dating Shelley Karlsen. Shelley was cute, but Cam could have dated practically any girl on campus. The more stunning model-types, for instance, the ones who drove around campus in convertibles with the top down and miraculously never got their hair messed up. But Cam had asked Shelley out instead.

And he hadn't asked her out until *after* I'd found that disk. I remembered, we had left the library with the wrong disk and gone straight to Burgers, Etc. He could have come back to the lab, discovered the mistake then, seen my name on the label of my disk, and followed us to the diner. Seen us together. Asked Shelley out just to get information about me, to get close to me, get that disk back without arousing suspicion. Hadn't she told me he wanted to get to know me?

Then he must have changed his mind about doing it that way, thinking it would take too long, and decided to take a faster, sneakier route by searching our room and vandalizing my car instead. But he'd stuck with Shelley the whole time. Because he still needed to know how much I'd discovered about the disk. Shelley was his way to do that.

He'd heard Shelley say I couldn't decipher anything. But he hadn't dared take her word for it. There was always a chance that she might be wrong. He couldn't afford to take that chance.

My eyes went to Cam's back as he bent over Shelley. He was holding her hand and talking to her in a soothing voice.

I moved closer. I wanted to see her face as she looked up at him. I wanted to see what was in her eyes.

They were terrified. She couldn't talk, but she was looking up at him and there was absolute, raw terror in her face.

Not wanting to believe it, I went over everything in my head. She had said he was going to join them in the bleachers after he ran his race on the day of The Games. Before he'd done that, had he flung that discus into my path? Then, in all the confusion as my friends ran down to the track, had he stolen my purse?

But . . . in the library just now, inside Nightmare Hall, he'd been sitting with Shelley. How could he have set off the smoke alarm?

I had no idea. Maybe he'd done something

to it earlier. He was smart. Like Donovan, Cam was majoring in electronics engineering. He could have figured out some way to make the alarm go off when he wasn't even near it.

The ambulance arrived and Shelley, fully conscious now, was loaded onto a stretcher.

I made Donovan drive me into town right behind the ambulance. I wasn't leaving Shelley's side, not while Cameron Truro was anywhere near her.

I didn't tell Donovan I suspected Cam. Cam was a friend of his, and I had no proof, yet.

I would keep this particular theory to myself until I knew more.

Besides, if I told Donovan, and he told Cam . . . I was already in danger. Why make it worse?

What I absolutely did *not* understand was why *anyone*, Cam included, would want to hurt Shelley. Take her life.

I kept my eyes on Cam the whole time they were checking Shelley in one of the emergency rooms, and later when they brought her out on a wheeled table and sent her up to a private room where they would "observe" her overnight. I never let him get any closer to her than I was. He didn't seem to notice.

Shelley's face was still an unhealthy shade of gray, the rims of her eyelids red, as if some veins had hemorrhaged, her lower lip still slightly tinged with a bluish tone. But she was awake and she was whispering in a hoarse, breathless voice, and I was grateful for that much.

I had to see her alone. I'd do all the talking, since it was clearly painful for her, but I had to tell her what I suspected about Cam. Who had a better right to know than Shelley?

I didn't want to hurt her. I'd have to be careful.

But the chance to share my suspicions about Cam with Shelley never came.

Because when she was settled in her room and I had made everyone else leave and told the nurse in no uncertain terms that *I* wasn't leaving, I was staying the night (she gave in when I whispered, "Her mother ran out on her and I'm not going to do the same thing"), closed the door, and sat down in a straight-backed wooden chair beside Shelley's bed, she surprised me by whispering, *"I have to talk to you. Don't say anything. Don't say a word until I've told the whole thing, or I'll lose my nerve. Just listen, okay?"*

Chapter 19

"*It was last Halloween,*" Shelley whispered. I had to lean close to the bed to hear her.

"Shelley, don't tell me this now," I said. My throat hurt just listening to her, she had to struggle so to speak. The doctor had told her not to talk. "You can tell me tomorrow. I'm staying the night, so I'll be here in the morning. Can't this wait until then?"

She shook her head vigorously. "*No. You have to know now. I should have told you sooner, but I couldn't. I thought you'd hate me.*"

She began again. "*It was last Halloween. You were going to a party with Brigham, one I wasn't invited to. I didn't want to stay home alone, with my dad moping around the house, so earlier that week I rented a costume just as if I were going to a party. I told the woman at the shop that I'd been invited to Cathy Anne*"

Younger's big Halloween party, which was a lie. But she didn't know that. I rented an angel's costume, with a mask and wings and a gold halo.

"I thought Cathy Anne should have invited me. I mean, we weren't good friends, but we knew each other, and a lot of people I knew were going. I figured since I had a mask on, no one would know who I was or that I hadn't been invited. So I crashed."

No big deal. We'd crashed parties before, Shelley and I. Everyone did it. It wasn't like people in high school sent out formal invitations. And who was going to be rude enough to toss you out on your ear after you were already inside?

"Everyone was in costume, so I didn't know who anyone else was, either. It was kind of fun, for a while. I danced and ate and was glad I wasn't sitting at home alone. But then Cathy decided she was bored, and suggested that we all go downtown to the Halloween parade on Sixth Street in our costumes. Everyone else was going, and I wasn't ready to go home, so I just jumped into one of the cars and went along."

Her voice gave out, and she gestured toward the table for a drink of water. I gave it to her, and when, with great effort, she had swallowed the water, she began whispering again.

"*It was really crowded downtown,*" she told me. She wasn't looking at me. Her eyes were on the white blanket covering her. Her fingers nervously played with its binding. "*I didn't really like it, although some of the costumes were neat. But it was too loud and too wild. People had been drinking, you could tell. There was a lot of loud music and shouting. Everyone else got really into it right away, but I was wishing I hadn't come. There was something scary about being in the middle of so many people.*

"*Then we ran into this bunch of guys from that private school on the south side. Cathy Anne said they were all snobs, and then a couple of guys in our crowd started making comments, and all of a sudden everyone was name-calling back and forth. I don't know who came up with the idea, but someone dared three of the guys, who were wearing Three Musketeers costumes, to climb a utility pole over in the next block.*"

Shelley had been given some pain medication for her sore throat, and now her voice took on a dreamy quality and I could see her eyes beginning to glaze a little. I was afraid she wouldn't be able to finish the story before she fell asleep, so I gave her another drink of water, hoping to keep her awake. I didn't want her to stop now.

The water seemed to revive her. *"I never thought they'd do it. Maybe they'd been drinking, I don't know. Anyway, the next thing I knew, we were all trooping over to the next corner, away from the celebration, and everyone was yelling at these guys to climb the pole, climb the pole, so the three of them put their hats, those big hats with the feathers in them, on the ground and began climbing. The poles have those metal footholds on them, that's how they got up there.*

"And everyone below was shouting and screaming and yelling at them to keep going, keep going, even when they got up so high, I was dizzy just looking up at them. One guy, the middle climber, lost his footing at one point and almost fell." Shelley's voice grew weaker again. *"I should have gone home then. But I didn't."* She turned her head from side to side, her eyes closed. *"Oh, Addie, I wish I had! I wish I had!"*

I knew I should make her stop talking. The doctor had said . . . but I couldn't stop her now.

"They went all the way to the top. At least, the first one did. The second one was just below him, and the third one farther down. They were yelling in triumph, and the one at the top let

go of the pole with one hand and raised his arm high in the air, as if he'd just won a boxing match." Shelley's head moved in agony again and this time when her eyes closed, they stayed closed, and tears began sliding down her face. When she spoke again, her voice was extremely agitated. "And his arm hit a high tension wire!"

I gasped in horror.

"There was this horrible flash of light or something, something bright, and he screamed, or maybe the guy below him screamed, and then there was this awful zapping sound, it only lasted a second, but it was awful, Addie, and the people around me were screaming and shouting and crying, and I stopped watching then because I couldn't stand it and I put my hands over my ears so I couldn't hear anything, only I still could, I could hear the guys on the pole shouting and shouting for someone to help them, help them, and I hear it now, all the time, when I'm asleep and even when I'm awake sometimes."

I could see the picture Shelley was painting with her whispers, and it sickened and horrified me. And I was only seeing that picture secondhand. She had been *right there*.

No wonder she was crying.

"The guy at the top finally fell. I didn't see

it, *but I heard the screams from the crowd and I heard the thudding sound when he landed on the grass at the foot of the pole. And just a few seconds later, there was another sound just like that when the second guy, who someone told me later had been reaching out to grab the guy on the top as he fell, lost his grip and fell, too.*"

She was crying harder now, and she stopped talking.

"What happened to them?" I couldn't help asking.

She didn't answer for a while. I thought she'd fallen asleep. Then she whispered, "*Dead. Both of them. The first one electrocuted, the second broke his neck when he fell.*"

"And the third one?"

She shook her head. "*He fell, too. But he wasn't up as high. So he wasn't killed. I heard later that he was in a wheelchair, that he'd never walk again.*"

She fell silent again. "*Then, I ran all the way home. I couldn't stand to be there another second. I never told anyone I was there, that it was my fault as much as it was anyone else's. I didn't go to school for a week. And I didn't listen to the news or read the paper, because I didn't want to know who they were. I didn't want to know their names. I thought that would make it so much worse, knowing their names.*"

"I remember that week. You said you had the flu." I'd heard about the incident, but I'd never connected it to Shelley's illness. I hadn't known anyone from that private school, so I didn't pay any attention to their names. Couldn't remember them now. "Shelley, how could you not tell me? I thought we told each other everything."

Fresh tears flowed. She couldn't seem to stop. *"I knew you'd hate me. It was terrible, what we did, awful! Two people died, Addie, and another one's life was ruined. I didn't want anyone to ever know that I'd been there, so I tried really hard to act normal. But I couldn't eat, I couldn't sleep . . ."*

That's why she'd lost all that weight.

And I hadn't noticed because I was head over heels in love with Brigham.

I sat there, watching her cry helplessly, my heart aching for her. The thought, when it came, came slowly, as most of my thoughts do. Shelley's name had been on that list, after all, along with others. A list of victims someone had to hate. I hadn't known why they were hated. Maybe I did now.

"Shelley?" I spoke gently, carefully. "Do you know if Donald Jacobs or Bob Printz were at that party?"

She didn't open her eyes. *"Everyone was in*

costume. *No one knew who anyone was. But Bob was probably there. He was a friend of Cathy Anne's. I don't know about Donald."*

Cathy Anne. Cathy Anne Younger. CAY. I had just deciphered the last set of initials.

"Is Cathy Anne at Salem?"

"What? Oh, Addie, I don't know. She could be. I haven't run into her, but she could be. Why are you asking me all these questions?"

"I just wondered. Go to sleep now, Shelley." She'd told me everything she knew about that awful night. And I had some heavy-duty thinking to do.

She reached out one hand to me. *"You don't think I'm a terrible person?"*

I felt tears of my own burning my eyes. "Shelley, you didn't do anything wrong. And I wouldn't have hated you if you'd told me then, either. I wish you had." She would have, I was convinced, if I hadn't been so preoccupied with Brigham.

Still, a part of me was glad that I had been, too. Because if I hadn't gone with him to a different party, I would have been with Shelley at Cathy Anne Younger's, and I would have gone downtown and I would have seen two boys die and another become paralyzed. I wasn't sorry I had missed that.

Shelley shouldn't blame herself. It was, after all, a crowd mentality. Besides, no one had intended such harm. It was an accident.

An accident. It must have been called that at the time. Was that why the author of the victim list seemed so determined to make his own attacks look accidental? Except for Shelley's, of course. The goal was the same, though: making attempted murder look like something else.

The creator of such a vengeful plan must have been a close friend of the three boys. A *very* close friend, filled now with rage and bitterness. And out for revenge.

Which meant . . . which meant that it couldn't be Cameron Truro. Because he wasn't *from* Braddock, or anywhere in the area. He was from Nassau County, New York. Somewhere on Long Island.

Or so he'd said.

Whoever it was, they had no right to mete out their own justice. Shelley hadn't done anything wrong. No one had. The boys didn't have to climb that pole. No one forced them. And it was no one's fault that the boy at the top had raised his arm in victory, encountering that deadly wire.

What had happened was horrible. But it

didn't deserve this kind of vengeance.

"Are you sure you don't hate me?" Shelley asked me one more time.

"No, I do not hate you. Now go to sleep, you need your rest."

In a few minutes, her breathing had evened out, and I knew she had obeyed.

I sat back in the chair, pulled the list of victims out of my jeans pocket, and placed it on my lap.

I was still weak with shock and anxiety, but my brain refused to take a break.

How had the friend of those three boys learned the identities of the people standing at the foot of the pole, taunting them, urging them ever upward? First of all, the victims weren't *from* our high school. Second, Shelley said everyone was in costume. No one knew who anyone was, although I was pretty sure really good friends would have known what the other was wearing.

And where was Cathy Anne Younger now? If she was here, at Salem, I had to warn her. Her name was on that list. And she was the only one left who hadn't been attacked. Yet . . .

It was late. There wouldn't be anyone at the administration building now.

I didn't want to wait until morning. There

was a telephone on Shelley's bedside table. First, I used it to call Donovan. When I had assured him that Shelley was okay, I asked him if he knew anyone named Cathy Anne Younger.

"Did," he corrected, "did know. She was in my political science class. Short, blonde hair, dimples?"

That was Cathy Anne. I had envied those dimples all through school. "*Did* know?" I asked him.

"Dropped out. So I heard, anyway. Hasn't been to class in a week. Prof Maynard asked if anyone knew where she was, and some girl said Cathy was pledging Omega Phi but hadn't been to a meeting at the sorority house in the past week, either."

We talked a few minutes more, then I said I didn't want to disturb Shelley and hung up. I didn't tell him the story she'd told me. Donovan was from Harrisburg. The story wouldn't mean anything to him.

Then I used the phone to call information in Braddock and get the Youngers' telephone number.

I told Cathy Anne's mother that I was a friend of hers from high school and I was wondering if she was attending Salem University.

"She went there, all right," the woman said,

her voice cold. "Not that we've heard from her. She doesn't keep in touch. We just pay the bills. I don't know," she added, sighing heavily, "we gave that girl everything and look how she treats us. Not a word from her. And after all we've done for her."

I hung up. Cathy Anne wasn't attending classes and she hadn't gone back home.

Where *was* she?

A chill swept over me then, even though the room was very warm. Because I was suddenly very terrified that I knew what the "DD" alongside her name on the list meant.

Dead.

Chapter 20

I worked on the code for hours. I did it by playing my own version of hangman, that game that television's *Wheel of Fortune* is based on. Filling letters into the blanks to create a word. I already had a head start because I now knew all of the names.

DMJ: Donald M. Jacobs. "Potsy." CRD. I wrote the letters on a paper towel, leaving spaces between them and then filling the empty spaces with vowels until I thought a word made sense.

It didn't take that long. How smart could a person be who signs the wrong name to a fake suicide note? Not half as smart as he thought he was.

CRD was easy. "Crowd" . . . the crowd at the bus stop, making it difficult if not impossible for anyone to notice who pushed Potsy. SHBAX was harder. I figured that out by picturing in my mind the scene at the curb that day. "SH" . . . shuttle. B . . . bus. Shuttle bus. AX . . . accident. SHBAX was nothing more than "Shuttle bus accident." And NIXQSSKD became "No questions asked."

He had counted on that, hadn't he? Make it look like an accident, and there will be no questions asked.

And if he hadn't got Shelley's name wrong, there wouldn't have been any questions asked then, either.

RLP: Robert L. Printz. The plan for him? Well, it helped that I already knew what had happened to him. MWRAX . . . "Mower accident." MNT MN BLD . . . at first, I thought the BLD stood for Blood, because there had been so much of it. But when I put it together with a bunch of a's and i's, it became, "Maintenance Man Blamed." Correct. It happened exactly as it had been planned.

How smug he must have been when that maintenance man had been led away!

CAY: Cathy Anne Younger. DD. I'd already decided that stood for "Dead." I hoped I was wrong. NIXQSSKD. Already deciphered. Whatever he'd done to her, he again anticipated no questions being asked, so he must have made it look like an accident.

And then there was Shelley. MC. Wrong.

NHSS, had to be Nightmare Hall, Study Session, which made my flesh crawl, because how could he have known she was going there? FKSCD . . . "Fake suicide." NT . . . "note." The FIN, I guessed, meant Finish.

He wasn't finished. The note in my lap was from the disk *before* I'd confiscated it. I was sure that by now, he'd added one more name.

Mine.

If I hadn't been so terrified, I'd have been a little smug, I think. I had decoded the entire list. By myself. Without anyone's help.

I couldn't think about that now. I had to decide what to do. He'd be looking for me. If Cathy Anne Younger was no longer alive and he was finished with everyone else on that list, I was the only one left. He couldn't let me live. How could he? I was the only person on campus besides him who had read the contents of that disk.

Did I have enough information to take to the police? I could start with Cathy Anne. They'd contact the administration and find out if she actually had dropped out. If she hadn't, wouldn't they begin looking for her?

Until then, where would I be safe?

The door to Shelley's room didn't lock. It was one of those large, heavy doors that swing inward, and there was no way to bar it. If I put a chair in front of it, one push from outside and the chair would topple to the floor. No help there.

But I was in a hospital. There were people out in the halls. Nurses, doctors, orderlies, maintenance help. I was safe here, wasn't I?

There had been people around Potsy, people around Bob Printz, and they hadn't been safe, had they?

I wasn't going to leave Shelley. He might decide he needed to come back and finish her off. But I wanted company.

I picked up the phone again, and this time I called Brynne. It was very late, and I knew she would whine and complain about how she hated hospitals, but she'd come. We'd sit out the night together, and in the morning I would go into Twin Falls to the police station, show them the code, and tell them what I thought it meant. Cathy Anne had been missing for more than seventy-two hours, so they would have to look for her. If they found her dead, they would know I was right about the code. And then they'd *do* something.

All I had to do was get through this one night safely.

Brynne finally agreed to come.

"Bring a pizza," I told her. I hadn't eaten in hours, and I needed to stay alert.

I tried. But the low blood sugar, combined with exhaustion, made me so light-headed, I had to close my eyes. I knew, oh, I knew that it wasn't a good idea. But I couldn't help it.

I was almost asleep when I heard the door creaking open and I smelled the unmistakable aroma of tomato sauce and spices.

My eyes flew open. But it wasn't Brynne.

It was Cameron Truro.

He was cradling a pizza box, and he was smiling that gorgeous smile at me. "Hey, Addie, I brought you sustenance. Brynne said you were starving. Hospital food's not so great, right?" He moved on into the room. "How's Shelley doing?"

I jumped out of my chair and began backing toward the bed, keeping my eyes on him. "Fine. She's just fine. Asleep. Where's Brynne? I thought she was coming."

"Chickened out. She really does hate hospitals. Some people are like that. Can't help it, I guess."

I'd kill . . . I'd let Brynne have it the next time I saw her. If I ever saw her again.

Which I might not. Because I didn't believe that Cameron Truro was from Long Island. Shelley had said he was rich, hadn't she? Rich enough to attend private school. But not on Long Island. Had to have been in Braddock, side by side with those boys who had fallen from the utility pole. It was *his* plaid shirt I'd seen on that arm near Potsy Jacobs just before he fell in front of the shuttle bus, and it hadn't been a helping hand he'd been extending. It had been a death weapon.

I knew why he was here.

He probably hadn't had any trouble convincing Brynne that he should come to the hospital instead of her. She hadn't wanted to come in the first place, and she didn't suspect him of anything, so why not let him do her this favor? What a great guy.

I couldn't think. I needed food. But I didn't want *his* food. "What about drinks?" I said. "There's a soda machine in the lobby. Would you mind?"

His eyes narrowed. He plopped the pizza box on the dresser just inside the door and glanced around the room. "You don't have anything to drink in here?"

"No. I didn't want to leave Shelley."

"Right. Well . . . I guess I should have thought to bring drinks. I'll get them. Just take a minute." But before he left, he fixed his eyes on me and said, "Anything wrong, Addie? You seem jumpy."

I uttered a short, stupid laugh. "Well! Who wouldn't be?" I said, gesturing toward Shelley as if to say, "After what happened tonight."

He nodded. "Yeah, right. Be right back."

The minute he was out the door. I whirled and grabbed the phone. I couldn't wait until tomorrow morning to call the police. I needed them *now*.

I had dialed only a nine and a one when the door creaked again. But before I could turn around, a rough, strong hand came over my mouth, another grabbed me around the waist, and a voice whispered in my ear, "Now, you don't want to do that, Addie."

Chapter 21

Before he yanked the phone away from me, the tip of my left index finger pressed down, hard, on the second "one." In the next instant, he ripped the phone away from me and flung it. It landed on Shelley's bed, out of my reach.

Pinioning my hands behind my back with one of his, he grabbed a white towel off the table in front of me and draped it over my head. I couldn't see anything but the floor and my feet.

"C'mon, let's go for a nice little walk," he said coaxingly. When I balked, planting my feet firmly on the white tile floor, he twisted my right arm behind my back and turned me toward the door, pushing, whispering in my ear, "There's no one out there. I checked. They're taking their midnight coffee break. No one can see us, Addie. Isn't that nice? Now, what we're going to do is, we're going to take a few short steps into the express elevator, which is right outside this room, and then we're going to go down to the basement, leave this hospital and go for a little walk. No one is going to see us, and you're not going to make a sound. Because if you do, I will snap your neck into a dozen tiny little splinters of bone, and then I'll come back up here and do the same to your friend in that bed there instead of waiting until later. Got that straight?"

I nodded silently, and did exactly as he'd said. Because I knew he meant every word. What was one more victim to him?

In spite of the towel over my head, I could tell when we left the building. I felt the cool air, and the sounds were different, although that late at night, the campus was fairly quiet. I heard a screech owl somewhere, and tires murmuring up the highway on the edge of the campus and car doors slamming in the parking lot.

Someone will see us, I told myself as he shuffled me along, my arm still twisted behind my back, my eyes still blinded by the towel. Someone will come along. I'll scream and run.

But no one came along. I heard no footsteps, no shouted hellos, no sound of anyone on the campus walkway but us. Me. And Cameron Truro.

"Shelley really likes you," I said bitterly.

"How could you do what you did to her?"

"Shelley is a fool," he hissed in my ear. "She never even told me her real name. That oversight on her part could have spoiled everything. That, and *you*."

I hated him for what he'd done to Shelley. Not just the fake suicide. He was going to break her heart, and Shelley couldn't afford that. It would set her back two-and-a-half years. "It's your own fault," I snarled. "Considering how important that disk is, you were an idiot to leave it behind in the library. And then you were even more stupid when you didn't just come and trade with me."

Furious, he yanked on the arm behind my back. I let out a squeal of pain. "I couldn't be sure you hadn't already looked at my file," he said, his voice low. "How could I take that chance?"

Then we were inside again. The cool air and the outside night noises disappeared, and we were surrounded by the silence of an empty building. Too quiet to be a dorm, even this late at night, and it didn't smell like the library. He pushed me forward, I heard elevator doors slide shut, and then we were gliding up, up, up. We stopped, the doors opened, we got out, and I was pushed again, into what felt like another elevator. Then we went up again, got out again.

I knew where we were, then. The Tower. Had to be. It was the only building on campus tall enough to require two elevators. One went midway, the other to the top floor, twenty stories up.

We had to be on the twentieth floor, because we'd taken both elevators. "I don't want to be up here," I said from beneath the towel.

"Good. I don't want you to like it."

We began moving again, also up, but this time on stairs. Impossible. Weren't we already on the twentieth floor? How could we still be going up?

Realizing then what our destination had to be, I refused to move. "The bell tower?" I asked breathlessly. "You're taking me to the bell tower? No, you can't. I won't go. I won't!"

The giant, metal bell, an authentic antique from a cathedral in London, hung in the middle of the very top of the tower. It rang automatically twice a day, once early in the morning, and once at twilight. It was surrounded by a narrow wooden deck, used only by maintenance men when a glitch developed in the computerized mechanism that rang the bell. The stone archways on all four sides were open to the birds and the bats and the wind and the rain.

It had been impressed upon us at orientation that the bell tower was *not* an observation deck and that it was off-limits to all.

Because it was dangerous.

Because one could *fall* from those open archways.

And I knew then that that was exactly what Cameron had in mind.

When I balked, he gave me a rude shove, knocking me to my knees. "Get up," he hissed, "or I'll knock you silly and carry you!"

I got up. And I continued to climb. "What did you do to Cathy Anne Younger?" I said.

"Aha!" he cried from behind me, "so you did figure out the code, after all. Shelley was wrong, wasn't she? Well, good for you. Doesn't matter now, anyway. And as a reward for your perseverance and intelligence . . . Younger was the worst of the lot. It was her idea to dare my friends to climb that pole. She egged everyone else on, and no one had the guts to defy her. She was vain and silly and stupid and arrogant and she deserved what she got."

"She's dead, isn't she? I know she is. That's what the DD after her name meant."

He laughed. "Wrong. It meant 'done deal.' I inserted that after her name last week."

"What happened to her?" I persisted, my breath coming in short gasps now. How many stairs *were* there? The staircase was very narrow. I could feel walls on both sides of me. I was so dizzy, I was terrified that I would fall all the way back down and lie at the bottom helpless while he finished me off.

The last step! I could feel the wooden deck beneath my feet as I stumbled onto it. The wind whooshing through the archways tore at my hair and slapped my cheeks with very cold air. I reached out for something to grab to steady myself, and my hands closed around a rope. The bell rope? No longer in use, but when I tugged gently on it with my free hand, I realized it was still attached to something.

Cameron was right behind me, still holding my other arm behind my back. He pushed up against me on the narrow walkway. "Where is Cathy?" I repeated over the howl of the wind around us. "What did you do to her?"

"She went into the river in her car," he cried, his voice distorted by the howl. "Very careless of her. When they find her, it'll look like an accident. But it wasn't, I promise you that."

The wind was slamming into me repeatedly, and I was being battered against the stone wall with almost as much force as in the lake. My empty stomach sent wave after wave of dizziness to my head. He was behind me, but an open archway was just to the left of me, and I fought desperately to stop swaying.

"I'm not really a student here, you know," he told me then, his mouth close to my ear. "I sit in on a few classes, but I'm not registered. I hung around at registration to see who my targets — that's what I was calling them — were befriending, so I'd know who to befriend to get close to them. But I never registered. With you and Shelley taken care of, I'm off and running, to another school, another list of targets. This was only Phase I. There were a lot of people under that utility pole, Addie. A *lot*. They went to different colleges. But I'll track them all down, sooner or later. I've got two dead best friends and one who can't get over his bitterness about what happened so he doesn't have a real life, either. I promised them, all three of them, that I'd pay back those people who sent them up that pole, and that's what I'm going to do."

"You're going to kill *all* of them?" I shouted. "All of them? Twenty, thirty, forty people, however many there were?"

"Only eighteen," he shouted back. "The rest of them had the good sense to leave when they saw what was happening. But not Younger. Not Printz or Jacobs or your good friend Shelley. They stayed. They had fun. And for that, they have to be punished.

"Don't you want to know how I found out who they all were?" The wind had picked up, its howl increasing until I could barely hear him.

I shook my head. "No!" I shouted, "I don't want to know any of it!" I couldn't believe I had ever wanted to know.

"After the funerals, I went to the costume shops in town. There are two of them, remember, Addie? I didn't have any luck in the first. But at the second one, the woman there is so paranoid about her business that when anyone rents a costume, she makes them write down where they're going to be wearing it. Insists on knowing where her inventory is at all times. She keeps very detailed lists. Who they are, which costume they're wearing, their addresses, phone numbers. I could actually have taken care of these people back in Braddock, but I knew that would be too risky."

Shaking, shivering, tears from the wind and from terror streaming down my cheeks, I shouted, "But if you saw Shelley's name on that list, you knew her name wasn't Michelle."

"Uh-uh. She just *told* the owner her name, and the woman wrote it down. What she wrote was, 'Michelle Carlson.'"

I really didn't want to hear any more. But as long as he was shouting in my ear, I was still alive. "And the smoke alarm?"

"I was sitting right beside the fireplace. There's a smoke alarm right there, which makes sense when you think about it. Everyone was busy studying, and no one noticed a thing when I held a lighter behind my back, right up underneath the alarm until it went off."

I was picturing the study session. And something was wrong with the picture. "No, you weren't," I said, turning my towel-draped face toward him as if I could see him. "You weren't sitting on the floor next to the fireplace. You and Shelley were on the couch, I remember."

No answer.

"Cameron? You weren't *on* the floor. I was, and Brynne, and Kirk . . ."

"The names of my friends who are dead now," the voice shouted, so close to my ear that I could feel his breath, "were Andrew Kirk and Sam Howard. Kirk and Howard. Get it? And you can take the towel off now, Addie."

I didn't have to. Before my freezing cold free hand could reach up and remove the towel, he did it for me.

I could tell by the look on his face that he was expecting me to be surprised. But of course I wasn't. Hadn't he just already told me who he was?

Not Cameron.

"My real name is Parker," the boy I'd met as Kirk Howard said to me, his very familiar face still close to mine. "Parker Nordstrum. But that'll be our little secret, right, Addie? No one will ever know. Because you won't be around to tell them."

He let go of my arm and pushed me sideways and back until I found myself teetering on the edge of one of the open archways, my arms desperately clutching the thick stone sides, the vicious wind pulling and tugging at me as if it were insisting that I join it out there.

Grinning, Kirk — Parker — tossed the white towel that had been on my head out through the archway next to mine. I was too paralyzed with fear to look, but in my mind, I could see it being tugged and tossed by the wind and then floating down, down, down . . .

And I could tell by the maniacal gleam in his eyes that I was about to follow it.

Chapter 22

"You think I'm going to push you, don't you?" he yelled at me.

I couldn't nod. I couldn't move. I couldn't breathe.

"Well, I have a better idea." He moved a few inches to the right, toward a round red button on the wall. "This button overrides the automatic pulley that rings the bell. Just in case there's a special occasion and the powers-that-be decide to ring the bell more than twice a day. All I have to do is push it, and the bell will swing your way. You are positioned in exactly the right place for the bell to knock you right out of that archway and let you fly. Haven't you always wanted to fly, Addie?" The wind blew his dark, shaggy hair around his face. He had to keep wiping it away from his face to look at me.

He *wanted* to look at me. He wanted to see

the terror in my eyes, wanted to see me suffer. And I hadn't even *been* at the foot of that telephone pole.

As if he'd read my mind, he tilted his head and shouted, "No, you weren't there. But you took my disk. How could I let you live, even if you hadn't cracked the code? But you did. Big mistake, Addie."

"I copied it, you know," I said. I didn't yell it, I just said it in a normal tone of voice. The wind suddenly died down, so that he heard every word. "I thought it was mine, and I needed a copy for Professor Nardo. She always asks for a copy of a work in progress." He wasn't a student, after all, so he couldn't know I was lying.

Doubt filled his wide, square face. "You're lying."

"I'm not lying. I was in a hurry. I just stuck it into the computer and made a copy before I even checked out the disk. Didn't know it wasn't mine." It was much easier to talk now, with the wind dozing.

He still had one hand near the button.

I knew what he was thinking. He couldn't be sure I was telling the truth, but if he killed me, and there was a copy of his file somewhere, he might not get to Phase II. "Where is it?" he demanded, taking a threatening step forward.

I couldn't do this. I couldn't. I wasn't clever enough or agile enough or smart enough.

But . . . I *had* figured out the code, hadn't I? Not just anyone could have.

"Where *is* it?" he screamed again.

I let my eyes drop from his face to the right-hand pocket of my jeans and then quickly lifted them again, as if I hadn't meant to look and was sorry that I had.

His eyes lit up, and he grinned without humor. An evil grin. "You've got it on you, don't you? Of course you do! You wouldn't keep it in your purse after I stole it at the stadium, and you wouldn't keep it in your car, you don't even have your car now, and you'd never trust anyone else with it. You'd keep it with you at all times. Give it to me!"

Oh, God, how was I ever going to pull this off? The tiniest mistake in timing, and we would both go out the window to our deaths.

"Come and get it!" I said defiantly, trying to keep my eyes on him and on the hanging rope just to the right of me, at the same time. I needed that rope. Without it, I was dead.

Hell, I was probably dead, anyway.

"You witch!" he screamed. But now he believed that I had it, and he wanted it back more than he wanted to punish me. He had more people to kill or maim, many more, and if I fell to my death with the disk that he thought I had in my pocket still on me, he would never get to finish his self-appointed task.

I knew that he intended to yank the disk out of my jeans pocket and then push me to my death.

"Come and get it," I repeated, "if you dare."

The word "dare," used so freely on that fateful Halloween night a year ago, made him go berserk. With a roar of rage, he lunged at me.

And at what I hoped, prayed fervently, was precisely the right moment, I threw myself sideways toward the hanging rope, grasping it with both hands. Gasping, crying, shaking, I hung there.

Without me in the archway to act as a barrier, he flew out the opening and down, down, down. Instead of me.

The wind had resumed its howling again around the bell tower.

So if Parker Nordstrum screamed on his way to his death, the sound was lost to me as I hung, frozen in fear, above the deck surrounding the giant antique bell.

Epilogue

We were walking across campus, Donovan and I, Cameron and Shelley, on our way to a dance at the rec hall. Shelley was wearing the red silk blouse, and she looked beautiful. And happy. She had spent the preceding weekend on Long Island Sound with Cameron and his family, and had come back to campus smiling. She was even thinking about answering one of her mother's letters, which had been piling up in a desk drawer for a year and a half.

We were getting closer to the Tower. Approaching it still made my knees go weak and my heart pound with terror, but I no longer went out of my way to avoid it. That was progress, I thought.

Sometimes the "ifs" got to me. If Cameron hadn't picked up the telephone lying on Shelley's bed when he returned to her room, hadn't heard a dispatcher on the other end repeating,

"What is your emergency, please, I can't keep this line open much longer, do you have an emergency?" and realized I had been placing a call to the police, if Shelley hadn't awakened then, figured out what had happened, I would have clung to that bell rope until my fingers couldn't hold on anymore and then I would have fallen through the opening between the deck and the bell to my death.

It seemed so ironic that it was Cameron who found me, when he was the one I had suspected all along.

I didn't want to feel sorry for Kirk — Parker — but I couldn't help it. He had been there that night, had seen what happened, had been helpless to save his best friends. It must have been horrible, watching two of them die and one of them maimed for life. Horrible enough to make your mind snap.

Still, he had done terrible things.

What was weird was, I hadn't liked the attention I got after it was all over. There was a piece in the campus newspaper about how I'd decoded the message, but when I read it, I hadn't felt anything. Nothing at all. It didn't seem important. I mean, *I* knew I had done it, knew now that I *could* do something like that. So I didn't really need to have anyone else know.

"Don't look at it," Donovan said, misreading the expression on my face as we passed the Tower. "Look at me instead."

I did look up at him. But I said, "It's okay, Donovan. It's really okay."

And it was.

About the Author

"Writing tales of horror makes it hard to convince people that I'm a nice, gentle person," says **Diane Hoh**.

"So what's a nice woman like me doing scaring people?

"Discovering the fearful side of life: what makes the heart pound, the adrenaline flow, the breath catch in the throat. And hoping always that the reader is having a frightfully good time, too."

Diane Hoh grew up in Warren, Pennsylvania. Since then, she has lived in New York, Colorado, and North Carolina, before settling in Austin, Texas. "Reading and writing take up most of my life," says Hoh, "along with family, music, and gardening." Her other horror novels include *Funhouse*, *The Accident*, *The Invitation*, *The Fever*, and *The Train*.

Return to Nightmare Hall
if you dare . . .

Kidnapped

Dark.

Dark and dim and cold.

Not like home.

Home. So hard to remember.

Why haven't they come to get me? Don't they want me anymore? Was I bad?

I wasn't bad. They should come get me. I don't want to be here. I hate this place.

I hate them for not coming to find me.

If they don't come, I'll hate them more.

Forever.

If they don't come, I'll punish them.

I will.